6/07

"Just looking forward to my day's work," she said blandly

"Job satisfaction is a wonderful thing."

"Isn't it? And by the way," he added, "what have you done to your hair?"

"Oh, I had it cut," Beth said cautiously. Had her triumph been short-lived? "I fancied a change," she mumbled vaguely when he didn't say anything.

"You've succeeded," he said. "From where I'm standing, you've succeeded very well indeed."

CATHY WILLIAMS is Trinidadian and was brought up on the twin islands of Trinidad and Tobago. She was awarded a scholarship to study in Britain, and went to Exeter University in 1975 to continue her studies into the great loves of her life: languages and literature. It was there that Cathy met her husband, Richard. Since they married, Cathy has lived in England, originally in the Thames Valley but now in the Midlands. Cathy and Richard have two small daughters.

CATHY WILLIAMS

Charade of the Heart

Harlequin Books

TORONTO • NEW YORK • LONDON
AMSTERDAM • PARIS • SYDNEY • HAMBURG
STOCKHOLM • ATHENS • TOKYO • MILAN
MADRID • WARSAW • BUDAPEST • AUCKLAND

ISBN 0-373-18605-3

CHARADE OF THE HEART

Copyright © 1992 by Cathy Williams.

First North American Publication 1995.

CHAPTER ONE

BETH looked carefully at her sister and counted to ten. It was difficult, but she wanted to find exactly the right words to explain, without resorting to downright exasperation, that there was absolutely no way she was even going to contemplate taking part in this juvenile scheme.

They had reached an age when these sorts of escapades should long have been left behind. When on earth was Laura ever going to grow up? It was tiring always being the one to frown and nod sagely and act reasonable.

'Well?' Laura prompted. 'What do you think?'

Have you got a few days to spare? Beth asked herself. She looked at her sister's flushed face, framed by the tangle of long auburn hair, and sighed.

'It's the craziest idea you've ever come up with,' she said, with what she considered a huge amount of restraint, 'and there's no chance that you're going to get me involved with it. I would rather spend the rest of my life in a snake pit. So you can wipe that grin off your face and leave my lunch alone.'

They were sitting in her kitchen, a cosy yellow room with pale, speckled wallpaper and matching curtains which had taken Beth ages to make. She tapped her sister's hand, which had been making surreptitious inroads into her plate of salad, and considered the matter resolutely closed.

'Oh, Beth.' Laura slipped out of her chair and went around to her sister, folding her arms around her neck.

'It's not that crazy, really it isn't, not when you think about it. And it's the only thing I can think of.' Beth could hear the tears in her sister's voice and hardened her heart. Laura had the knack of turning the tears on with alarming ease and she wasn't going to fall for it. Not this time.

She bit into a lettuce leaf liberally soaked with salad cream and didn't say a word.

'You're mad,' she muttered finally, disengaging herself from her sister's stranglehold and clearing away the table.

Laura followed her to the kitchen sink and dipped her finger into the basin of soapy water, trailing it into circular patterns, her long hair hanging forward and hiding her face.

'You're so unsympathetic,' she muttered. 'Here I am, in the worst fix in my life, and you're not prepared to do anything at all to help. I was counting on you, Beth. Why do you think I drove all the way up here in this weather? If I had known that you wouldn't give me the time of day, then I'd have stayed at home and...and...' Her voice trembled, and Beth sighed again.

'I'm not unsympathetic,' she said gently. 'Stunned perhaps, but not unsympathetic. I mean, how on earth could you have let yourself become pregnant? Don't tell me that it just slipped your mind that there are about a million types of contraceptives available.'

She eyed the half-completed washing-up with resignation and led her sister into the lounge.

Like the kitchen, it was small, but imaginatively furnished. Beth's job as secretary-cum-book-keeper in a small electronics company didn't pay that much. It was all she could do to meet the mortgage on her tiny two-bedroomed flat. But it was hers and she had decorated it as tastefully as she could on a minuscule budget.

Whenever she felt like giving up, she told herself that things would improve as soon as she had completed her accountancy course and could find herself a better job. All that studying she had to do in her free time would pay dividends.

By nature she was an optimist. Didn't they say that every cloud had a silver lining?

Laura had collapsed on to one of the chairs and was hugging a cushion. A picture of misery. Beth looked at her doubtfully. This didn't seem like any act, although it was hard to tell. Laura had the ability to look woebegone if the weather report began with showers and light snow.

'Look,' Beth said calmly, 'there's no point weeping and wailing. You're pregnant, with no chance of marrying the father of the child. You'll just have to do what anyone else in your situation would do. Work for as long as you can and then leave. You've said that you can't go back to the job as you haven't been there long enough to qualify for maternity leave. So what? It's hardly the end of the world.'

She bit back the temptation to lecture on the sheer insanity of becoming involved with a married man, not to mention becoming pregnant by him. Her sister had enough problems on her plate without that.

From the sound of it, though, Beth could think of a thousand better places to put her loyalty than with a creep who had knowingly involved himself with Laura when his responsibilities lay elsewhere. He didn't know about the pregnancy but she seriously doubted that that would have influenced his actions. He had left her sister high and dry after a three-month fling. A baby on the way was hardly likely to have changed that.

Couldn't Laura have suspected the sort of man he was?

'It's the end of the world for me,' Laura said, in between sobs. Beth handed her a box of tissues. 'Jobs like mine don't grow on trees, you know. I love it there. It pays more than I could ever hope to get in a lifetime of doing secretarial work.'

'Then you should have thought about all that before you got yourself into this situation.'

'How was I to know that David...' there was another onslaught of weeping and she blew her nose noisily into a tissue '...that David was married? He didn't tell me until he decided to walk out. And by then it was too late. I was already pregnant. And I'm still in love with him,' she finished miserably.

'Surely not,' Beth said, aghast.

'I knew you wouldn't understand.' There was an edge of accusation in Laura's voice now. 'You've never been in love. Not even with Craig. It's easy for you to sit there and sound horrified just because I haven't had the common sense to have acted the way you would have done! You don't know what it's like! You've always been so sensible. When Dad died, you were the one who was strong enough to support Mum, and when she remarried you were the one who told me not to cry because that would only make her unhappy, and, when they both went to Australia to live last year, you were the one who waved them off at the airport and told me that life had to go on!'

Beth felt the prick of tears behind her eyes. Laura had managed to make her sound like a monster, but she was practical, that was all. Was that some sort of crime? As for Craig...she preferred not to dwell on that and pushed it to the back of her mind. Easy enough to do. Laura was right about that, at any rate. She hadn't been in love with him, had felt no fireworks. When he had broken off their relationship she had been upset, but not distraught, had picked up the pieces and carried on. It was the only way, wasn't it?

Now her sister had sprung this latest escapade on her, and had expected... what?

She had spent a lifetime reacting in the only way she had known how to her sister's recklessness. Now that control, that inability to become involved, had become as much part of her as the colour of her hair or the shape of her nose.

'You're being unfair!' she protested uncomfortably.

'No, I'm not. You don't want to understand. In a minute you'll start telling me to pull myself together.'

'I just don't know what to do,' Beth objected. 'I'm not some sort of miracle-worker. I understand, honestly, and I'll help in whatever way I can, you know that. I'll baby-sit, I'll buy things for it, as much as I can afford, I'll even sell my flat and move up to London to be closer to you. What more do you want me to say?'

Silly question. Beth waited for the inevitable response.

'You know how you can help me, if you really want to,' Laura insisted stubbornly. There were smudges on her face from where the tears had dried, giving her a fragile, pathetic appearance.

'It wouldn't work,' Beth said helplessly, but there was less determination in her voice now, and Laura sensed it, moving in like a shark that had scented blood and was homing in for the kill.

'It could work,' she said earnestly, moving forward closer, impatiently sweeping her hair away from her face. 'Come with me, I'll show you.'

She stood up and held out her hand. Beth reluctantly took it, allowing herself to be led into the bedroom. Like a lamb to the slaughter.

Laura guided her to the tall mirror that stood next to the dressing-table in the bedroom.

Outside the wind was fierce and relentless, rattling the window-panes ever so slightly. It was a perfectly dark night, the moon obscured by the dense layers of cloud that had hung over the country for the past few days.

Inside, the bedside lamps threw patterns of light and shadow across the room and the overhead light with its pretty apricot shade picked out the figures of the sisters, illuminating them.

Beth looked silently at their reflections, seeing them through Laura's eyes and reluctantly understanding what had inspired her sister's hare-brained plan.

Two women, both the same height, both the same shape, both with the same oval faces and luminous green eyes. Identical twins.

She was the first to look away, throwing herself on to the bed and staring sightlessly up at the ceiling.

Trading places. It had been a ridiculous game when they were children, but they weren't children now. They were women in their early twenties, and surely the time for ridiculous games was over?

Laura sat on the bed, her knees pulled up to her chin.

'Please, Beth, do it for me. It can work. I'm sure of it. Would I jeopardise my whole life if I didn't believe that?'

You're mad enough, Beth felt tempted to say.

'My boss would never notice,' she continued persuasively. 'He's hardly ever there. He owns a string of hotels worldwide, not to mention enough other business interests that keep him out of the country for weeks on end. My orders tend to come by phone or fax. And when he is around he's always far too busy to notice me other than in the capacity of the secretary who follows his dictates.'

'Sounds a treasure,' Beth said drily.

'You know what I mean. He breathes, eats and sleeps work. No, maybe not sleeps. He has enough women around to fulfil him on that score.'

'Charming.'

'But what I'm saying to you is this: we don't have the sort of close working relationship that would make him notice any difference if you replaced me. He probably wouldn't even see that our hairstyles were different and, if he did, you could tell him that you had had your hair cut.'

'And you like working for this man?' Beth sat up, propping her head on her elbow and staring curiously at her sister. The man hardly sounded like a comfortable type to be around.

'I love it. I've never had so much responsibility in a job in my life before. That's why I'm so desperate to hang on to it. As far as I'm concerned, working for Marcos Adrino is the best thing that ever happened to me. That——' she patted her stomach '—and the baby. It's all I have left of David, and I'm happy with that.'

'Oh, yes, the baby. So I'm to cunningly replace you at the Adrino corporation, not arousing so much as a whisker of suspicion, while you move into my flat and temp until the baby's born, and then what?'

'And then,' Laura elaborated, her eyes positively gleaming now that victory was tantalisingly within reach, 'and then I move back up to London and take up where you left off. My friend Katie is a professional child-minder. She's already promised to look after it.'

'Convenient.'

'Yes, it is,' Laura agreed, unaware of the oblique sarcasm in her sister's voice.

'And how do I cope with all those little details like knowing the layout of the office? The filing system?' Why, Beth wondered, am I actually allowing my curiosity to encourage Laura in her mad ideas?

'I'll fill you in on that. It all runs remarkably smoothly. Marcos told me when I first applied for the job that the secret of a successful office lay in its simplicity. Everything documented and on computer so that no one was indispensable to the company.'

'Except him, of course.'

'Right.' Laura's voice was full of awe.

The man obviously had something, Beth thought, although from where she was sitting that something sounded very much like a healthy dose of arrogance.

'And don't you think that other people might notice our little swap?'

'Not likely. Marcos's office occupies the top floor of the building, and there are only a handful of people there. The two vice-presidents who work for him, and their secretaries, whom I have very little to do with.'

She rattled off their names and Beth held up her hand to staunch the flow of information.

'And what about my job?' she asked. 'Do I just tell them that I'm taking seven months' leave to help my sister out in a scheme that could have come straight out of a third-rate movie, but to hang on, I'll be back?'

'You quit.'

'I quit.'

'Sure. Why not? You know that you're only there because it's convenient and because it helps pay the mortgage. I can get a temp job somewhere and pay your mortgage, and you can use my huge salary for the next seven months to build up that little nest-egg you're always telling me you wish you had.'

'I see.'

Beth could hardly credit her sister with the fore-thought she had taken in preparing the ground plan of all this. For every question, she had an answer, and all of the answers were logical in a bizarre way.

'Besides,' Laura continued, 'you told me how much you'd like to get out of here for a bit, to put a little distance between you and Craig. Here's your chance.'

'It was wishful thinking!' Beth objected weakly. 'Besides, I've got over all that.'

'Have you?'

Beth looked at her sister and sighed. She knew what lay behind this piercing concern for her emotional well-being. It had little to do with the state of her heart and much more to do with the fact that it would fit in very nicely with her plans, thank you very much.

'Yes,' she said firmly, 'I have. I don't look like someone on the verge of a nervous breakdown, do I? I'm quite grateful to him in a way; he taught me a valuable lesson about the male species. They're best left alone.'

She had enjoyed an undemanding relationship with Craig for seven months before he'd left her for someone else. Men like that, she had decided, instilled caution when it came to the rest of their sex. She wouldn't be getting involved with another man for a very long time indeed, and she could have told her sister that dragging up that unfortunate episode and tacking it on to her arguments was useless.

She didn't, though. Talking about Craig still made her feel vaguely disillusioned, and Beth preferred not to dwell on anything that served no purpose other than to depress her.

Instead she offered her own counter-argument. 'And Mum? Do you think that Mum will give this little venture her blessing?'

Laura sat upright and adopted a complacent expression which sent chills down Beth's spine. It was the same expression she had seen whenever her sister was about to confront a problem with an irrefutably foolproof answer.

'That's the beauty of it,' she said smugly. 'You know how Mum's always spent her life tearing her hair over me. In fact, she still does that now, even if it is only by letter. Well, I won't tell her about the pregnancy just yet. I'll fill her in just before the baby's due, and by the time she arrives the swap will be accomplished, and I'll be back in my job. Easy.'

Beth shook her head wonderingly. 'Is it all worth it?' she asked.

'For me, yes. I know you're content to stay in the hicks here, studying by night, working by day to pay the bills, but it's not for me. I love London. I love my job. I don't want to own a cosy little place. Not yet.'

Beth groaned.

'And when the baby arrives?' she asked. 'You're going to have to settle down, Laura. Babies and the wild single life don't exactly go hand in hand.'

Laura's eyes shifted away from her sister's face. 'Time enough to think about that.'

What other answer had she seriously expected? Beth thought. Laura had always lived on the premise that the future was a bridge to be crossed when you came to it. While *she* had worked hard towards building something for herself, Laura had run through a series of unsatisfactory jobs, never thinking of tomorrow.

'The wonderful thing is,' Laura was saying, her voice low and urgent, 'I've been at the Adrino corporation for six months now. Long enough to know that it's the only job for me, but not so long that I know too much for you to catch up on. Right now, I'm doing pretty routine work, even if I do have the freedom to prioritise it the way I want, and you would be able to slot in with no trouble at all. And if you don't understand anything, no one will be too surprised if you ask questions.'

'Including your boss?'

'Just so long as you only ask the question once,' Laura replied truthfully. 'He has the sort of brilliant mind that grasps things immediately, and he expects everyone who works for him to do the same.'

This sounded worse and worse. The man was an ogre. Beth could picture him without too much trouble. An arrogant tycoon, someone with a receding hairline and a bit of a paunch, testimony to stress and business lunches, but with enough money to attract whatever bimbo his heart desired.

'Please,' Laura wheedled, creeping up the bed to hold her sister's hand. 'If you hate it there, I promise I'll do what you want. I'll admit that I'm pregnant and I'll work my notice and then leave. What have you got to lose?'

Beth hesitated, and Laura immediately seized the opportunity.

'And the rest up here will do me good,' she said fervently. 'I'll be able to do some thinking, and I'll get away from London for a while. There are too many memories for me in London. We could both do with swapping places for our health.'

'That's emotional blackmail,' Beth pointed out wearily.

But the battle was over, and by the time they finally switched off the lights she was already coming to terms with the fact that she was either as crazy as her sister or else so lacking in will-power that she had allowed herself to agree with something which bore all the resemblance of a jaunt in a minefield.

Laura had taken a week off work, and they spent the time laboriously going over the routines in the Adrino corporation. She had brought one of the company magazines with her, and she pointed out all the faces of the people Beth would meet and would have to recognise.

They weren't that many, mostly the people who worked in the higher echelons of the company. It was a fortunate coincidence that her sister had not been in London long enough to acquire her usual following of male admirers. Her closest friend was Katie, who was aware of the plan.

David, she assured Beth with a note of bitterness, although he worked in the company, which was where she had met him, had applied and got a transfer abroad.

'Running as far away as he could from me,' she said with an attempt at bravado.

'Isn't that easier than if he had been around?' Beth enquired mildly, and her sister shrugged agreement.

By the end of the week, Laura had managed to find herself a temp job, but her work at the Adrino corporation had obviously spoiled her. She rattled off what she would have to do now and was clearly appalled by the prospect.

Beth tactfully refrained from another lecture on it all being her fault, and that as she had made her bed, so would she have to lie on it.

She herself had successfully managed to resign from her job without having to give the obligatory one-month notice. She had pleaded an unfortunate family matter and tactfully left it to her boss to decipher whatever he wanted from that obscure statement.

It had hurt a lot less than she had expected. Had she really spent so much time in a job that she had shed without too many tears? Or maybe it was the stirrings of what was awaiting her.

Laura had made the whole scheme sound like a marvellous adventure, but the following Monday morning, as Beth stood outside the impressive Adrino building, she felt far from adventurous.

She felt an impostor, dressed in her sister's jade-green suit. Was there a law against this sort of thing? she wondered.

She smoothed her hair back nervously and chewed on her lip. All around her people rushed past, lots of little soldier ants hurrying to their jobs.

A dull sun was attempting to break the stranglehold of grey clouds but it was easy to see that it was a losing battle.

She felt a light spitting of rain and merged into the line of soldier ants, finding herself swept into the massive building.

If I don't look at anyone, she thought, then I won't risk ignoring any recognisable faces.

But she was perspiring with nerves as the lift whooshed up to the top floor, disgorging her into the plushest set of offices she had ever seen in her life before.

The carpet was of muted grey-blue and thick enough to make footsteps soundless. The offices lay behind smoke-coloured glass.

One of the secretaries looked up as she walked past and waved, and Beth waved back. Marian, secretary to Ron Wood, the financial director.

'Nice week off?' Marian asked, stopping her in her tracks, and Beth smiled and nodded.

'A little eventful,' she said, inwardly grinning at the accuracy of the description, 'but relaxing on the whole.'

'Good. I wish I had a week off coming up. I'm up to my ears in it. You've had your hair cut?'

Beth ran her fingers self-consciously through her bob. 'Spur-of-the-moment,' she said vaguely.

'Suits you. Makes you look more businesslike. Not,' Marian continued hurriedly, 'that you didn't look great with long hair.'

Beth accepted the compliment with a smile. She liked Marian straight away. She was in her middle thirties, tending towards plumpness and quite plain to look at with her short wavy brown hair and spectacles, until she smiled. Then her face lit up and was really very attractive.

'See you later, anyway,' she said with another wave, and Beth nodded, walking confidently towards her office which she knew was at the end of the corridor.

First hurdle, she thought, successfully manoeuvred and out of the way. It surely couldn't be as simple as this. Life was never that simple. It always insisted on throwing in a few complications to making the going more interesting.

But right now her self-confidence was a notch higher.

There would be a stack of typing awaiting her—she knew that from what Laura had explained—but that would be no problem. She had spent a long time working with the same computer system.

She pushed open the door to her office and gasped.

It was a large room, carpeted in the same shade of muted grey, but the walls were covered by an elegant dove-grey wallpaper. Her desk was an impressive mahogany affair, and the filing cabinets, also in mahogany, were stacked neatly against the wall.

Opposite, a large abstract painting dominated the wall. It wasn't the sort of thing she would have chosen herself, but she decided that she rather liked it. It was soothing.

Marcos Adrino had probably hand-picked it. She had had to revise some of her ideas on his appearance. From the picture in the company magazine, he was younger than she had originally thought, but she had no doubt that the paunch was still there. The handful of wealthy men she had met had all seemed to be slightly overweight. Products of too much access to rich food.

She hung her coat on the coat-stand and settled comfortably into her chair, browsing through the pile of letters, most of which she could tell at a glance, from experience, simply needed filing. Faxed letters from the boss were awaiting typing.

Beth looked at the strong, aggressive handwriting and felt a twinge of relief that he wasn't around. She could do with a few days breaking in before she faced him.

She switched on the computer terminal and was about to begin working on the first letter when the door behind her opened.

She heard his voice before she saw him. It was deep, and right now tinged with enough hardness to freeze her to the spot.

'Here at last. In my office. Now.'

She swivelled around to see him vanishing back into his room, and her head began to throb with nerves.

One day into this, and already things weren't going to plan. He was not supposed to be here today. He was supposed to spend most of his time out of the country. In fact, from what Laura had told her, he was supposed to be in Paris and Geneva until the end of the week. At least. So what on earth was he doing here?

She licked her lips nervously and wished that she had listened to her good sense and laughed her sister right out of town.

He was standing by the window waiting for her, his body negligently leaning against the sill, one hand thrust into his trouser-pocket.

The difference between the man in front of her and the one she had conjured up was so vast that she looked away in confusion.

Marcos Adrino was tall and, far from having a paunch, he had not a spare ounce of fat to be seen. In fact, he had the body of a superbly tuned athlete, broad-shouldered and lean-hipped. A body that looked powerful, even though it was covered by an expensively tailored charcoal-grey suit.

Beth cleared her throat and looked at him, taking in the hard, clever lines of his face, the black hair, the dark, penetrating eyes, the curve of his mouth.

Pull yourself together, girl, she told herself. You're the sensible one, remember?

He was staring at her through narrowed eyes.

'Sit down,' he ordered abruptly.

Beth edged over to the chair and sat down, lowering her eyes to her shorthand pad, making an effort to steady her hand.

It wouldn't do to look ill-at-ease. She got the feeling that this man picked up things like that, processed them through his shrewd brain, and always came up with the right answer.

He remained standing where he was and she looked up at him with a bright smile.

'I didn't expect you,' she said in a businesslike voice.

'I dare say you didn't,' he drawled.

'Successful trip?'

'It would have been, if I hadn't been privy to certain rumours circulating.'

'Rumours?'

She managed a weak smile.

'Rumour number one has it that you've been shirking your responsibilities here,' he said coldly. 'I don't pay you to waltz into this office any time you feel like it.'

Beth gathered her wits together. This wasn't a dictating session at all. She should have guessed that the minute she saw that forbidding expression on his face.

'I didn't realise that I had been,' she ventured.

'Really.' He moved over to his chair and sat in it, inclining back, his hands clasped behind his head. 'In that case, you don't seem to be aware of the time you're supposed to get here. I can assure you that it's not ten o'clock.'

His voice was smooth and razor-sharp, and Beth looked at him with dislike. She had been spot-on when she had read arrogance behind her sister's description of her boss. It was stamped all over him, but she was damned if he was going to stamp it all over her.

'If I've been late on a couple of occasions,' she said coolly, 'then I apologise. It won't happen again.'

'It had better not. You've exhausted your first chance with me. Next time it happens and you don't provide an acceptable excuse, you're out. Understand?'

Beth swallowed her anger.

'And what excuse would you consider acceptable?' she asked with interest, forgetting that she was supposed to be holding on to her sister's job and not kissing it sweet goodbye through the window. 'Death, perhaps?'

Marcos's mouth narrowed to a thin line.

'Nor do I pay you to give me lip, is that clear?' He stared at her and Beth defiantly met his gaze.

'I'm sorry,' she muttered, fiddling with her pad.

This man was more than merely uncomfortable to be around. He was unbearable, and if Laura had been around she would quite happily have strangled her on the spot.

'Have you prepared the groundwork on the St Lucian project?' he asked, changing the subject.

He was trying to catch her out. Beth could sense it instinctively and she thanked her lucky stars that Laura had filled her in on all the details of the major jobs he was working on.

The St Lucian project involved an immense lot of work concerning the construction of an exclusive complex in St Lucia, the sort of complex that catered for the sort of people who never associated holidays with cost.

'Yes,' she responded calmly. 'The groundwork's all been covered and an appointment with the Minister of Tourism is scheduled for next week.'

It felt good to reel off the right answer. Marcos Adrino would have had no hesitation in reducing her to the size of a pea had she not been able to meet his question with an adequate response.

She got the feeling that he had no compunction when it came to eliminating dead wood from his company. Or, for that matter, from his life. She considered what her sister had told her about his private affairs, about the women who were drawn to him like iron filings to a magnet. Now, seeing him, she realised that he was the kind of man who treated women as disposable playthings. Men, she thought, she could well do without, and this breed of man was particularly on the objectionable list.

'I do feel, however,' she said, throwing in her own opinion on what Laura had told her about the project, 'that more care should be taken to involve the visitors into the island life. A fabulous complex is one thing, but it can be enhanced by easy access to the local customs.'

'You have opinions now, have you?' he asked softly. 'And since when has your efficiency extended beyond my orders?'

Beth didn't answer. She would have to remember to act in character, and Laura would never have volunteered such an observation without being asked.

'Is that all?' she murmured, preparing to leave. 'Sir?'

'The name is Marcos,' he answered easily, 'use it. You always have. And no, as a matter of fact, that's not all. Not by a long shot.'

Beth waited and the silence built around her like an electric field.

He had something else to say, and, from the sound of this particular brand of silence, whatever it was it wasn't pleasant.

CHAPTER TWO

NEVER in her entire life had Beth felt so acutely ill at ease. And the worst part was, Marcos Adrino wasn't at all embarrassed at her discomfort. He continued to stare at her, those black eyes taking in absolutely everything, until she felt like jumping up from the chair and begging for forgiveness for whatever the hell it was she was supposed to have done, because he still hadn't said.

He would have made a great interrogator, she thought. He certainly had the ability to fill his silences with unspoken threat.

'I've been hearing other, slightly more distasteful rumours about you,' he broke the silence, but there was still a dangerous softness to his voice. He idly picked up the silver letter-opener from his desk, running the edge along his finger with caressing delicacy.

Did he have to do that? Beth wondered nervously. Was he doing it on purpose? She didn't think so. There was something absent-minded about his action, but even so, it was menacing.

No wonder, when Laura had spoken about him, her voice had been filled with awe.

Of course, she decided, falling back on her good, old-fashioned sense of practicality, any awe Laura felt towards him was totally misplaced. All that forbidding arrogance didn't intimidate her at all. Well, not now anyway. Maybe to start with, but she had got the measure of him now, she decided.

He had something unpleasant to say to her and, instead of just coming right out with it, which was what any normal boss would have done, he was playing a cat-and-mouse game with her. Creating a shroud of tension around her, waiting for her to snap, at which point he would no doubt find the whole scenario hugely entertaining.

'Oh, yes?' Beth asked politely.

His mouth hardened. Any minute now, she thought, and he'll tell me that I have an attitude problem. But she was damned if she was going to let Marcos Adrino walk all over her. He might treat the rest of the human race like that, but not her. Not if she had any say in the matter.

She fleetingly thought that she was supposed to be impersonating her sister and that Laura would never have dreamt of answering back to him, and promptly pushed the thought aside for future reference.

'You don't seem overly concerned,' he said, dropping the letter-knife and standing up.

Beth followed his movements warily as he walked around the desk to perch on it directly in front of her.

Another little ploy, she told herself. Designed to make the guilty party feel inferior and vulnerable. It won't work.

Her green eyes serenely met his, and she saw an expression of what? Puzzlement? Almost as though he was trying to figure something out. Then it was gone and he was looking at her with cold disapproval.

'Of course I'm interested in whatever rumours you've heard,' Beth agreed with the same level of controlled politeness in her voice. 'Not that rumours are always based on fact.'

'Your week off certainly seems to have turned you into a little philosopher,' Marcos observed coolly. 'I don't remember you being so opinionated before. Who did you spend the time with?'

'No one,' Beth said hurriedly.

'Not even David Ryan?'

So this is it, she thought, I might have guessed. Her face reddened and then just as quickly drained of all colour.

'I see that's managed to crack that controlled little façade of yours.'

'May I ask who has been spreading these...rumours?' she asked. Not that I'll be able to deny them. Laura, she groaned inwardly, why on earth did you have to fool around with someone in the company? Why couldn't you have contented yourself with any one of the hundreds of other men in London who had nothing at all to do with the Adrino corporation?

Marcos smiled coldly. 'I really don't think that's relevant, do you?'

'I suppose not,' Beth said dully.

'The fact is that you and Ryan have been sleeping together, haven't you?'

'I didn't realise that what I did outside of company time——'

'You know damn well that it's not allowed. You're my secretary and Ryan isn't just one of the junior members of staff. He's one of our directors.'

'He is?' She hadn't thought to ask Laura what David's status in the company was, and Laura had, naturally, tactfully omitted to mention it.

'Don't try and plead ignorance,' Marcos bit out. 'It won't work. I had noticed that his work was becoming sloppy. Is that why he requested a transfer to Paris?'

'I don't know. You'll have to ask him,' Beth hedged, looking away.

'I'm asking you. But don't worry, your face says it all for you. No doubt you drove the poor fellow into a corner and he fled from the country to get away from you.'

'I resent that!' she exclaimed hotly, standing up. It was on the tip of her tongue to inform him that she wasn't paid to sit in his office and be systematically insulted. That he could expect her resignation first thing in the morning. But, of course, she couldn't. Laura would never have forgiven her if their convoluted efforts to secure her job had lasted precisely two hours and had resulted in Beth walking out.

She bit back her words and rearranged her features into what she hoped was an expression of subdued apology.

'Sit back down,' Marcos commanded abruptly. 'You'll leave when I'm finished with you. You've been playing with Ryan, and who else? Is he one of a succession of men you've been sleeping with in my company?'

'No, of course not.'

'Because I won't have it. I can do without being known as someone who has a tramp for a secretary.'

'I am not a tramp!' Two bright patches of colour had appeared on her cheeks, and she realised that she was perspiring all over.

'I needn't tell you that rumours of your affair with Ryan could very quickly spread into rumours of an affair with me.'

The black eyes glinted cynically at her. She wondered briefly whether that wasn't bothering him as much as Laura's love-affair with David. After all, it was easy for

a boss to lose credibility with his staff if it was rumoured
that he was sleeping with his secretary.

And that would be quite an easy assumption to make.
He was attractive, she supposed, if you liked that sort
of ruthless appeal, and he was aware enough of his own
sexuality to realise that women were drawn to him.

'I can assure you that you don't need to fear anything
on that score,' she informed him stiffly.

'No?' He raised one eyebrow, and this time there was
a distinct gleam of lazy amusement in his eyes.

It altered the hard contours of his face totally, and
she caught a swift, disturbing glimpse of the sort of self-
assured charm that could knock any defenceless woman
for six.

But she was far from defenceless. Oh, no. She had
always been a controlled person, and since Craig she had
erected a good many barriers to protect her from ever
again being taken in by a few charming smiles and some
well-rehearsed chat-up lines. That glimpse of raw sex
appeal, she firmly told herself, stood no chance.

'No,' she told him.

'You mean you're not attracted to me?' There was
slightly more amusement in his eyes now, and it made
Beth angry. There had been nothing amusing in his accusations a minute ago and, if he thought that he could
dictate her responses to him by turning on a bit of mas-
culine charm, then he was in for an unpleasant surprise.

'That's right.' She stood up and smoothed her skirt,
then she bent to retrieve the shorthand pad and her
pencil. And not once did she even glance in his direction. 'Is that all, now?'

'That's all.' He moved across to the window and stood
staring broodingly out. The fine drizzle that had started
earlier in the morning had not let up. She could see the

persistent wetness clinging to the window-pane, as though the top of the building were stuck in the middle of a cloud.

She turned to go and halted at the door when she heard the deep timbre of his voice behind her.

'Just so long as we understand each other,' he said silkily. He had turned to face her, and Beth's mouth suddenly went dry. No wonder this man had such a high opinion of himself. He was clever, that much was apparent in his eyes, and he knew it. He was powerful, and he knew it. And he was sexy, and that he was certainly aware of.

But he wasn't perfect. If he were he would be able to see the stubborn hostility in her face.

'I think we do, Mr Adrino.'

'Marcos. I told you when you first got this job that everyone in the company was on a first-name basis.'

'So you did,' Beth murmured, unable to resist a smile as she thought that they had done it. They had really managed to pull the wool over Marcos Adrino's sharp eyes. They had fooled him. He didn't have a clue that the woman standing in front of him had never been interviewed by him for any job.

'Care to tell me what that smile on your face is all about?' he drawled. 'I can't imagine that the past hour has exactly filled you with a warm glow.'

You'd be surprised, Beth wanted to retort, still highly amused at the thought that she had fooled the infallible Marcos Adrino.

Her smile widened. 'Just looking forward to my day's work,' she said blandly. 'Job satisfaction is a wonderful thing.'

'Isn't it? And by the way,' he added, as she opened the door, 'what have you done to your hair?'

'Oh, I had it cut,' Beth said cautiously. Had her triumph been short-lived? 'I fancied a change,' she mumbled vaguely when he didn't say anything.

'You've succeeded,' he said, sticking his hands into his pockets. 'From where I'm standing, you've succeeded very well indeed.'

Beth stepped out of the office and shut the door firmly behind her. His words were ominously perspicacious. She really would have to remember that she couldn't give in to the temptation to react in the way she customarily would have done. That she and Laura, identical twins though they were, were very different as two individuals.

She almost fell into her chair with the relief of no longer being in Marcos's presence.

It hadn't just been his relentless accusations, she thought suddenly, as she logged into the computer and ran her eyes briefly over the huge store of files, realising that she would have to work a lot of overtime to really understand Laura's job fully.

There was something alarming about him. Maybe it was just that she was not accustomed to being confronted by a man who acted as though the whole world was designed to fall in with his orders.

Her little job in Cambridge had certainly not prepared her for this particular breed of man. Her own boss had been quite mild-mannered. A sympathetic middle-aged man with three children, all girls, who wore a look of perpetual harassment on his face. Whenever anyone joked to him about it, he would laugh and reply, what do you expect, living with four women?

Beth couldn't imagine that Marcos Adrino had ever been mild-mannered. He had probably been born arrogant. She tried to imagine him as a baby and found that she couldn't. The only image she could conjure up was that dark, devilish, ruthlessly handsome face.

She stuck a couple of horns and a tail on her mental image, chuckled and then settled into the laborious task of catching up with the outstanding workload of typing.

When Marcos next strode out of his office, he glanced across at her with surprise.

'Dieting?' he drawled, slinging on his coat and pausing to stand over her.

Immediately Beth felt her pulses begin to race.

'Pardon?'

'It's nearly two o'clock,' he told her, and she returned his curious stare with surprise.

'Is it?' she asked, consulting her watch and feeling unnervingly gauche and idiotic. 'Oh, yes, so it is. I must have become a bit involved.'

'So I see. Keep it up and you won't feel the sting of my disapproval again.'

'Yes, sir,' she replied tartly, wanting to hit him, and his lips curved into a small smile.

'I won't be back until tomorrow afternoon. I have two meetings tomorrow at Harlow and Ridgewood's. Last-minute arrangements; they probably won't be in your diary. Finish compiling the research into Santo Domingo, will you? I want to get all that off the ground by the end of the month. Latest. I take it you won't object to doing a bit of overtime to get it all cleared?'

'Of course not.' Had he really expected any other answer? The question had been phrased in such a way as to negate any other reply. Not that she had any objection to overtime anyway. For the salary that Laura was being paid, working long hours was more or less expected.

Not, she thought, that her sister had allowed that line of reasoning to enter her mind from what Marcos had told her. She would have to confront Laura with that.

He strode towards the door, and Beth subconsciously thought how graceful his movements were for someone of his height and powerful build. Stealthy, she corrected herself. Like a jungle animal. He probably slept with one eye open as well.

He paused just as he was about to leave and threw over his shoulder, 'By the way, if Angela calls, make some excuse. She's being a bit of a nuisance.'

With that he clicked the door behind him and Beth frowned. Angela? Who on earth was Angela? She was obviously meant to know who Angela was and was expected to dispatch her efficiently out of his life. Was this all in the line of duty? Ha!

She spent the remainder of the afternoon ploughing through the stack of dictated tapes and messages in her tray, occasionally breaking off to take phone calls and to rummage through the computer files, gradually building up a picture of Marcos's extensive business involvements.

There was much more to it than hotels, although they were by far the bulk of his business. Hotels spread across the world, from New York to Tokyo.

In addition he had investments in several electronics firms and software companies.

Had he built all this from nothing? Even if he had not, the man was clearly a dynamo in the concrete jungle.

When she next looked at her watch, it had gone seven o'clock and she hastily packed up. This, she reminded herself, was only a temporary excursion into the Adrino corporation. Filling in time until Laura could take over. It wouldn't do to start becoming too involved.

Now she understood why her sister had been so keen to keep her feet in the company.

She made her way back on the Underground to Laura's flat, which was in Swiss Cottage. It was a rented apartment. Very comfortable and large enough really for two people, but lacking in character. Nothing like her little place, but then you never had the incentive to do anything with property that did not belong to you, she supposed.

Laura, anyway, had never been terribly houseproud. While she could spend hours browsing in an antique shop, Laura had always been more than happy to flit from boutique to boutique, spending all her money on clothes.

And it showed, Beth thought wryly, as she prepared herself a light meal of tuna and French bread. Her sister's wardrobe was about five times the size of hers and the clothes were way out of her price range.

As soon as she had eaten, she telephoned her sister, waiting in frustration as she heard the flat ringing tone. Surely Laura wouldn't be out living it up, for heaven's sake? She hardly knew a soul in Cambridge. Beth herself only had a handful of good friends there. She had told them that she was going to be away for a while and that her sister would be looking after her flat, but none of them knew any of the details and she didn't care for the thought of Laura spilling them unwittingly.

Her train of thought was broken by Laura's voice at the end of the line.

'Beth,' she heard the voice distantly, and felt a sudden pang of longing to be back in her flat in Cambridge and far away from this dreadful affair. 'How was your first day at work?' There was a brief pause, then she continued anxiously, 'You made out all right, didn't you?'

'Oh, none of your colleagues recognised anything amiss,' Beth began. 'They commented on the change of hairstyle but that was about all, and I've been doing a lot of work getting myself up to the mark on your work.'

'You will remember that it's not permanent, won't you?'

Beth smiled. 'Of course I will. Believe me, working for Marcos Adrino, invigorating though the work might be, isn't my cup of tea.'

She heard her sister gasp down the line and her smile broadened. She could imagine Laura's expression of horror that she had been plunged into the deep end so suddenly.

'But he's not back in England until the end of the week,' she wailed.

'Well, then, he's obviously more unpredictable than you thought. He was there when I got in, and I don't have to tell you that I almost had a heart attack when I heard his voice from behind me.' She shivered involuntarily.

'What did you do? What did you say? You didn't give the game away, did you?' Laura's voice had risen to a panicky squeak.

'No, and don't get so excited, for heaven's sake. Not in your condition.' She sat down on the sofa, curling her legs underneath her, her eyes absent-mindedly wandering over the television which she had switched on earlier, having turned down the volume to make the phone call. It was a cheap thriller of some sort, and the entire cast seemed to be wearing expressions of either bewilderment or guilt.

'Well? Tell me all the details. Hang on, I'll just settle down here. Your cushions are so delicate. You need some great big ones on the floor.'

'Thanks, but try not to give in to the urge to redecorate my flat. You've done quite enough at the moment, what with redecorating my life.'

'So spill the beans. Tell all.'

'Laura,' Beth said bluntly, 'what the hell has been going on in that office with you?'

'What do you mean?'

'I mean the man laid into me the minute I was in his office. He said that you had been shirking your job, coming in late.'

'Oh.' There was a sheepish silence at the other end, then Laura burst out defensively, 'It only happened a couple of times.'

'A couple?'

'Well, four or five.'

Beth sighed. 'Well, he found out about the four or five times and he was livid.'

'Oh, dear. I wonder who told him? I had morning sickness. Honestly, Beth, I just couldn't drag myself into work on time, and I could hardly tell anyone, could I? I'm sorry. Although it's kind of a relief that you were there to handle him. I've heard that he can be positively scary when he's crossed. I would have just burst into tears, I know it. I've been very emotional since I got pregnant.'

'Thanks,' Beth commented wryly. 'But I can tell you I wished I'd never been talked into this insanity.'

'You're not going to back out, are you?' There was a hint of tears already in Laura's voice.

'No, but I want some honesty from you. This David character. Was he the only one? I mean...'

'Beth! How could you even imply...!'

'You can be a bit of a flirt,' she stated flatly, 'so don't play the innocent with me, my girl. Don't forget, I know you better than anyone else in the world. You've spent a lifetime mastering the art of getting yourself into scrapes with men, so don't act as though you're shocked by the question.'

'I haven't been sleeping around, if you must know,' Laura said with asperity. 'The minute I met David, that was it.'

'Good.' At least that was one less problem to worry about, Beth thought. She couldn't have coped with an entourage of men beating a path to the top floor whenever the coast was clear.

'What do you think of Marcos?' She heard her sister's voice and it was brimming over with curiosity.

'I've met more pleasant people in my time,' Beth answered firmly. 'He's every bit as arrogant as I expected him to be.'

'But attractive, wouldn't you say?'

'I suppose so,' Beth confessed grudgingly, remembering the feeling of hostility he had evoked in her, 'though not my type. He's too self-confident for his own good and he acts as though when he says jump he really expects the rest of the world to obey.'

'Oh, they do.'

I can believe it, Beth thought. She changed the topic. She didn't like talking about Marcos Adrino. It made her think of him, and thinking of him made her skin begin to prickle.

They chatted about what the weather was doing, Beth reminded Laura not to forget to water her plants and to collect a dress from the dry cleaners down the road, and it was only as she got into bed that she suddenly remembered Angela.

She had completely forgotten to ask Laura who the hell Angela was, and how she was supposed to handle her.

Then she decided that she didn't care anyway. As far as she could see, it wasn't part of her job description, or rather her sister's, to deal with Marcos's personal life, and if he didn't like it, then he could lump it.

She put it to the back of her mind and there it remained the following morning as she busied herself with her twin tasks of briefing herself on the company, including the project in Santo Domingo, and typing up the reports that had been left on her desk after she had gone home.

Marcos had obviously put in an appearance at the company, and it must have been late because he had been nowhere to be seen when she had left. He must run on overdrive, she thought.

She was relaxing over her fifteen-minute lunch break comprised of a cup of black coffee and an apple, when the door to her office was flung open and Marcos swept in, bringing with him that feeling of restless energy that she had seen the day before.

'I'll have one of those,' he said without stopping at her desk, 'in my office.'

He strode into his office, slamming the door behind him and Beth winced. A very good afternoon to you too, she mouthed, gulping down her last bite of apple and moving over to the percolator.

He was poring over some paperwork at his desk and he barely glanced up when she entered.

'Your coffee?' she reminded him of her presence.

He stared at the cup, then he stared at her. 'What the hell is that?'

'It's a cup of coffee,' she answered. What else could it be? A jug of orange juice?

'I don't take my coffee black. I take it white, with one teaspoon of sugar.' He leant back in his chair and scrutinised her. 'Surely you should know that by now?' he asked softly. 'You've really changed, and more than just your hairstyle. Am I missing something here? Am I being a bit dense?'

Beth retrieved the cup from the desk, steadying her nerves. She had automatically poured him the same coffee as she had herself. Stupid. Little oversights like this made this dangerous game as glaringly obvious as if she had committed some larger, more noticeable mistake.

'I'm sorry. My mind must have been elsewhere.'

'Either that, or you left it behind in Cambridge.'

'What?' Beth asked sharply, smiling to hide the sudden tension she felt.

'You went to stay with your sister, didn't you? Jane told me.'

'My sister?' Her mind was working furiously. Who, she wondered, was Jane? The office spy from the sounds of it, and office spies could be extremely dangerous.

'Something wrong with your hearing today, Laura?' he asked, his eyes narrowing suspiciously.

Beth smiled again. 'Of course I went to stay with my sister. In Cambridge.' She gave a little laugh. 'I would have gone somewhere more glamorous, but my funds were a little low at the time.' She would have to stop being so jumpy every time she thought that he was edging towards the truth. After all, there was no way that he could even suspect that Laura was miles away in her little flat, while she was here pretending to be someone she was not.

'Where would you have gone?' he asked curiously. 'I would have associated you a few weeks ago with somewhere on the French Riviera, close to a few nightclubs, but perhaps I misread you completely.'

Beth shrugged non-committally. She didn't like this sudden digression on to personal topics. There could be a lot of unexpected traps here. For a start, she didn't know what Laura had told him about herself, if anything, and he wasn't likely to dismiss another slip-up like the coffee. He was altogether too shrewd. His clever, calculating mind probably stored information that most normal people would forget within seconds. Stored it and had it quite handy to recall at a moment's notice.

'I've never been to the French Riviera,' Beth finally volunteered, as he continued to look at her from under his dark lashes. 'And I've never felt any particular wish to go, if you must know. In fact, I haven't done a great deal of travelling at all.'

'But you'd like to?' he prompted.

Beth fidgeted uncomfortably. She didn't like this. She was sure that he couldn't give two hoots whether she hated the idea of planes, or else saved madly to go on one. Laura had said that he barely noticed her except in her capacity as secretary. So why the sudden interest now? She wondered whether he suspected something odd, a little thought hovering somewhere at the back of his mind. A little thought that he was beginning to explore.

'Wouldn't everyone?' she answered distantly.

'No. I personally have seen enough of airports to last me a lifetime. Hotel life, you know, outstays its welcome very quickly.'

'Does it? I wouldn't know. Anyway, I'll make you a fresh cup of coffee now, if you like.'

'Why,' he drawled, 'do I get the impression that you're eager to get out of my company?'

His words, for reasons that she couldn't fathom, sent a hot flood of colour to her cheeks. Or maybe it was the way he had spoken them, in that lazy, slightly speculative voice.

Whatever, there was no answer to that question and she left the office quickly, only realising how tense she had been when she exhaled her breath deeply in the safety of her own room.

By the time she re-entered his office she was perfectly in control of her senses once again, and the cup of coffee was precisely how he liked it.

He began to talk to her about work and she breathed a sigh of relief. When he talked about work, she was on relatively safe ground.

As she was leaving his office, she turned around and said on the spur of the moment, 'Do you remember what you said to me about getting bored of hotel life very quickly?'

He looked up from his paperwork and nodded.

'Well,' Beth continued awkwardly, 'it's just a thought, but these projects in St Lucia and Santo Domingo—you could try and make them places that would never outstay their welcome.'

He looked at her assessingly.

'Any suggestions?'

Beth laughed genuinely. 'None at all. Don't forget I'm inexperienced enough to find any sort of hotel life quite a novelty.'

He looked as though he was about to say something, but when he finally did it was only to inform her briskly that she could apply herself to giving the matter some thought, then he returned to his paperwork.

Effective dismissal, Beth thought, letting herself out, but she felt suddenly invigorated.

She was absorbed in reading one of the folders on St Lucia when the outside door to her office opened. But it wasn't Marian, who normally peeped in with files or reports for Marcos.

This woman she had never seen before.

'Can I help you?' Beth asked, wondering how she had managed to bypass the usual security checks and make her way successfully to the top floor.

'Is Marcos around?' The woman smiled politely. She was very poised, every strand of blonde hair neatly tucked into a sophisticated chignon at the back of her neck.

'Who may I say is asking?'

'Oh, don't bother to announce me,' she said quickly, 'I'll let myself in.'

Before Beth could do anything to stop her, the woman had made her way to the connecting door, and Beth could just see Marcos's dark head look up, then the door was very firmly closed.

She returned to her work, but her mind was seething with questions.

Finally, and with a feeling of ridiculous surreptitiousness, she called Laura at her workplace, and said without preamble, 'A blonde woman just walked into Marcos's office. She didn't tell me who she was. Am I supposed to know?'

'Blonde?' Laura asked. 'Very leggy and very glamorous? Probably wearing silk or cashmere?'

'That's the one.' The woman had been dressed in a pale pink cashmere suit with a strand of pearls around her neck, and they didn't look like the synthetic stuff either.

'Remember I told you that Marcos is quite something with the women?'

'Yes,' Beth answered.

'Well, that's one of them. Angela Fordyce.' She groaned down the phone. 'He finished with her about three weeks ago, and under no circumstances were you supposed to let her in to see him!'

CHAPTER THREE

BETH tried to summon up the feeling of bravado she had had the previous day when she had resolutely decided that Marcos could handle his own damned personal life.

But sitting here, in front of her computer, her eyes flitting warily across to the connecting door, it was difficult.

She had already been subjected to his cold anger and it was something she had no desire to experience again.

She frowned at the file she had been poring over a minute before, but the words were just a jumble of black and white. Eventually she gave up.

She could, she thought, leave for home. It was already half-past five. She chewed her lip, glanced across at the door again and remained undecidedly rooted to her chair for another half an hour.

This is ridiculous, she finally decided. Hovering about here like some sort of criminal waiting to stand before the judge.

She stacked her papers away and unhooked her coat from the coat-stand. Now that she had decided to leave, her feet couldn't move fast enough, and by the time she made it to the ground floor she was positively churning with tension.

She only managed to regain some of her equilibrium on the Underground back to the flat, but even when she was safely indoors she found that she was plagued by the same sense of apprehension.

More alarmingly, her mind was fizzing over with questions that she knew shouldn't concern her at all.

Was that the type of woman he fancied? Tall and blonde and with the sort of impeccable good looks that spoke of hours painstakingly spent in front of the mirror? Angela Fordyce, she found herself thinking uncharitably, didn't look as though her brain had ever taxed itself with anything more complicated than whether her colour scheme for the day matched.

Not that it was any concern of hers anyway. The man was infinitely dislikeable, someone who constantly seemed to rub her up the wrong way. He was welcome to his following of leggy blondes. Peculiar though it might seen, they probably suited him. Men whose work lives ran on constant pressure no doubt found the company of brainless bimbos relaxing. They could unwind without the tiring obligation of actually having to respond to any manner of intelligent conversation.

She switched on the television, laughing at her line of thought. Am I really so bitchy? she wondered. She had never been before.

She had changed into a pair of tight jeans and a loose sweater and she had a sudden, unwelcome image of herself standing next to Angela Fordyce, her short bob hardly the most glamorous hairstyle in the world, her face bereft of any make-up, her feet inelegantly clad in a pair of thick woollen socks to stave off the cold.

With a little frown she shoved the image to the back of her mind and settled down to follow the detective movie. She liked detective movies. Something about them appealed to the logical processes in her brain. That was probably why she enjoyed the mathematical precision of her accountancy course. There was no room for emotive flights in an accountancy course. Things made sense with it. Two and two always added up to four.

Her mother once told her that it was a trait that she must have inherited from her father. He had possessed a fine mind, a mind that had enjoyed the precision of logic.

Laura, she had said, took after her. They were both volatile and emotional. Two and two, with a generous helping of imagination, sometimes added up to five.

Why, Beth thought pensively, had she suddenly remembered that? Was it because her cool, reasonable approach to life had recently been less reliable? Odd.

She refocused her attention on the small screen and was once again absorbed in various permutations of theory being volunteered by the chief detective, when there was a sharp knocking on the door.

She reluctantly got up, wondering who on earth it could be. Were there such things as door-to-door salesmen in London? Or maybe it was Katie. She had been meaning to get in touch with Katie, but hadn't found the time so far.

She pulled open the door and her body tensed immediately.

'Oh,' she said, simply because she couldn't find anything better to say, 'it's you.'

'Surprised?' Marcos walked past her into the small lounge, making no apology for his appearance even though it was after ten o'clock.

He stood in the centre of the room and stared with blatant curiosity around him.

Beth felt her hackles begin to rise.

'I thought only doctors paid home visits,' she said pointedly, shutting the door behind her. She would have preferred to leave it open, so that he could get the message that she really didn't want him in the flat, but it was simply too cold outside for that.

Now that the door was shut, she had a sudden feeling of choking claustrophobia.

'Funny,' he mused, 'I would have expected your flat to have more of an imprint of your personality on it. It looks as though you only use it as a place to sleep.'

'Have you come here for something specific?' Beth asked, reasserting her presence. She moved to the chair furthest away from him and sat primly on it, leaning forward slightly, her arms folded across her chest.

She was aware of her heart beating quickly and heavily. What was he doing here? He had obviously just come from work, he was still wearing his suit, although that didn't exactly speak volumes, did it? She had left him at the office with Angela; who knows what they had got up to? He might have finished with her, but men, she knew, were very susceptible to a beautiful and willing woman, even a beautiful and willing woman who had gone past her sell-by date.

'Why did you let her into the office?' He looked at her through half-closed eyes.

'What?'

'You heard. Angela. Why did you let her into my office when I expressly told you not to?'

Oh, so this is it, she thought. He couldn't even have the courtesy to wait until the morning before venting his anger.

She felt a stab of indignation. Some of that bravado that had eluded her earlier on was returning.

'I could hardly put her under civil arrest just because she wanted to see you, could I?'

'You could have told her that I was out,' he said forcefully. 'Or ill, or in a meeting. The list of excuses is endless. You've always managed to handle that sort of situation before.'

'Have I indeed?' So it was one of her unofficial duties, and one which her sister had happily complied with. Well, she had no intention of following suit.

'Yes, you damn well have,' he snapped.

'Well, as a matter of fact,' Beth informed him calmly, 'I don't see why I have to handle your personal life for you.'

'What?' he roared. He stood up and began pacing the room, running his fingers through his hair. Beth watched him without moving, fascinated. It was an effort to finally drag her eyes away and sternly remind herself of all those qualities he possessed which she thoroughly disliked.

'I said——'

'I heard what you said the first time.'

'Then, there's no problem, is there?'

'There damn well is! I don't like the implied criticism in your voice one bit! Have you forgotten that you're my secretary?'

This was quite a different sort of anger from the icy anger he had shown her when she had first arrived at the office. This was more like a thunderous rage.

Beth didn't see any reason why she should bend under its impact when he was exercising it in her flat. Or rather her sister's flat. Whatever.

'I've decided that my duties stop with my work,' she stated in a voice that was far more controlled than she actually felt.

'Oh, you've decided, have you?' Marcos asked smoothly. 'And since when? Since that overhaul you had on your week off? That damn sister of yours has a lot to answer for.'

Doesn't she just? Beth thought.

He paced across to where she was sitting, and before she could take defensive measures leaned over her, his hands gripping either side of her chair.

Beth felt herself automatically flinch back. This was way too close for comfort. He was making her giddy; something about his nearness overwhelmed her. It was almost an effort to breathe normally.

'I...' she began, then her mouth seemed to dry up and she found that she couldn't complete the sentence.

'I know what you think,' he said grimly, overriding anything she might have had to say. 'You've suddenly decided that it's all right to start passing moral judgements on my personal life.'

'I haven't decided any such thing,' she muttered weakly. She just wanted him to go away, now, even if it was only to another part of the room. He was too close, his arms only inches away from her breasts.

'You damn well have,' he shot back, his eyes glinting. 'As far as I'm concerned this little self-righteous act of yours doesn't cut any ice with me whatsoever. You're hardly eligible for the horrified virgin act, are you?'

His words were carefully placed. Without thinking, Beth raised her hand and slapped him angrily across the cheek, watching in horror as his face swivelled under the impact.

The hooded black eyes met hers with a gleam.

'That certainly hit home, didn't it?' he said softly.

'You're despicable.'

'At least I don't pretend to be what I'm not.'

His words, unthinkingly, were so accurate that Beth felt her face blanch.

'You've been sleeping around with Ryan and God knows how many other men, and you actually have the nerve to silently criticise me!'

There was no answer to that one.

'Moreover,' he continued, still leaning over her, stifling her with his proximity, 'I damn well ought to give you the sack for what you've just done.'

'Why don't you?' Beth challenged, throwing caution to the winds.

'God knows,' he muttered, standing up. She released her breath slowly as he moved away to stand next to the window.

She had saved Laura's job, if only by the skin of her teeth, and the thought should have made her feel elated, but it didn't. Something had changed, her control had slipped and that made her uneasy and a little bit frightened.

This was poetic justice, she thought, for having been stupid enough to take part in this monumental piece of deception in the first place.

'The fact is——' Marcos turned to face her '—I didn't really come here to talk about Angela in the first place. She's no longer part of my life anyway. No, I came here to ask you whether your passport's in order.'

'Pardon?' Beth's eyes opened wide. Things were moving way too fast for her liking.

'Your passport—is it in order?'

She nodded. 'Why do you ask?'

'Because you're coming to St Lucia with me.'

'I am?' she squeaked, suddenly realising that for some reason she couldn't fathom she didn't want to do that at all.

'You can book the flights tomorrow, and we'll fly on Thursday morning. I have a meeting arranged with my man over there that evening.'

'Thursday? This Thursday morning?' She knew that she must sound like a parrot, repeating everything he said, but their conversation was beginning to have an air of unreality about it.

'You really should have that hearing problem seen to,' he said sarcastically. 'This Thursday. Yes. You should be able to make all the arrangements in a day. I'll be out of the office.' He paused significantly. 'You said you wanted to travel, didn't you?' he drawled.

'Yes, but...' But not with you, she finished silently.

He was staring at her and he must have been reading her mind, because his next words were, 'You can relax. You won't be alone with me, not that I would have thought that you were intimidated by being thrown together with a member of the opposite sex. No, Jane will be coming with us.'

'Jane?' She decided to ignore his sarcastic remark at her expense. He could think what he liked of her from now on; she didn't care.

'Yes, Jane Morris,' he said impatiently. 'Marketing manager?'

'Of course. Jane.' The name rang a vague bell in her head now that she heard the surname. It must have been one of the names that Laura had mentioned when she had been filling her in on the company personnel.

'And in case you get any ideas,' he said, resuming his unnerving prowling around the room, 'this is a business trip. I don't intend to have to keep my eye on you.'

'Why would you have to do that?' Beth asked with genuine curiosity.

'Because,' he said, stopping to look down at her, 'from what I've heard you're not against, shall we say, promoting yourself at the first available opportunity?'

He smiled cynically and she had an irresistible urge to repeat her slap, but she controlled it. Instead she stared down at her fingers, not trusting herself to answer.

'Not going to see me to the door?' he asked, throwing his scarf around his neck.

Beth got up reluctantly, following him to the front door and keeping just enough distance between them so that her nervous system didn't start doing funny things again.

'You know something?' he said in a lazy voice, as he was about to leave. 'Out of work clothes, you're not at all what I had expected.' His eyes scanned her briefly, but Beth had the oddest sensation of having been stripped of her clothing. 'My character assessment of you was obviously wildly misplaced.'

With that parting shot, she watched him as he stepped quickly across to his car, a sleek Jaguar which had been slotted in between two contraptions that looked as though they had seen action in the First World War.

She waited until the car had sped off and was out of sight, then she slowly let herself back into the flat, shivering from the night air.

Her movements were leisurely as she cleared away her coffee-cup, undressed, slipped into her pyjamas, but her thoughts were tripping over each other.

An all-expenses-paid trip to the Caribbean should have sent her spirits zooming on to Cloud Nine, but she considered the prospect with growing apprehension.

Working with him was bad enough, but in St Lucia she would be in his presence without respite. Almost without respite, she amended. There was Jane Morris, whoever she might be.

She glanced at the bedside clock, wondering whether it was too late to telephone her sister and decided that pregnant women would definitely be a little put out by a phone call in the middle of the night.

Instead she flung open the wardrobe drawers and inspected Laura's supply of clothing.

At least, she thought wryly, she wouldn't have to rush out in her lunch hour and purchase a set of summer clothes. There were T-shirts of every hue, light dresses, shorts and swimsuits. She picked them up slowly. All bikinis. And the sort of bikinis that left very little to the imagination. Not a one-piece in sight. Well, it was too late to remedy that. They would have to do.

By the time she finally got into bed it was well into the early hours of the morning and she awakened six hours later feeling totally unrefreshed.

Outside, the sunshine had resolutely lost the battle it had been fighting for the past day or so, and it was raining furiously.

Lucky me. Tomorrow I'll be out of all this, she thought brightly, wishing she could feel slightly more enthusiastic.

Her thoughts were even gloomier one hour later when she arrived at the office.

She had spoken to Laura, had had to endure at least fifteen minutes of her shrieks of envy, and had then been informed that Jane Morris was not exactly the most congenial companion to be stuck with for a few days.

'She doesn't like me,' Laura had said emphatically. 'She's never liked me. I'm surprised she hasn't put in an appearance in Marcos's office as yet. She's always hovering around, like a bad smell, just itching to make some snide little dig at my expense. Maybe she got eaten up by her workload.'

'She can't be that bad,' Beth had protested in dismay, only to be informed that she was worse.

'She thinks I sleep around,' Laura had said casually, and Beth got the distinct impression that this little titbit had been deliberately saved until she was well and truly ensconced down here.

'Which you don't,' she had said wearily.

'Certainly not! I have to admit that I became quite friendly with some of the guys in the office, you know, had a few drinks now and then after work, but that was as far as it went. And once David came along, well...'

Quite friendly? A few drinks? Oh, God. Beth hadn't wanted to hear any more. She had rested her head on her hand, feeling like an unwary climber who had suddenly stumbled into thick fog.

Was it any wonder that there was just the tiniest whiff of a reputation surrounding her sister? Couldn't Laura ever handle herself with a bit of moderation?

And Fate didn't even have the compassion to comply with her plea that the plane be already fully booked.

She phoned through with the dates, her fingers crossed that the last-minute booking would ensure no seats, only to be told that she was very fortunate as they were travelling out of the tourist season so that there was no problem with the flight. Especially in the first class section. He quoted her a price and Beth gulped in shock.

'Can't take any more of this dreary English weather, eh?' the girl's voice down the other end joked.

'I can,' Beth replied seriously, 'but it's the boss's orders.'

'Would you like to swap jobs?'

Quicker than you can imagine, she thought.

At least she had been granted one day's reprieve from Marcos. She wouldn't be seeing him until the following morning at Gatwick Airport, nor, she was relieved to find, would she have to make the trip up with Jane. There was a memo waiting for her on the desk when she arrived to work that bluntly informed her that Jane would be overnighting in Reigate, so that Laura would have to find her own way to the airport.

During her lunch-hour, Beth darted out to the chemist's and bought herself some suntan oil and moisturising cream, and then spent the rest of the day trying to concentrate on her workload.

For once she left on the dot of five. There was packing to do, even though they would only be away for four days, and in between she fitted in her overdue telephone call to Katie.

She was astonished to discover what a relief it was to chat to someone who was aware of her true identity. In the background she could hear the sound of screaming children, and she grinned. Laura was in for a shock when she discovered that her bundle of joy was also a bundle of hard work.

But there was one thing to be grateful for. Katie sounded like a pleasant, down-to-earth person. They both amicably grumbled that taking part in Laura's scheme had been temporary insanity.

'She can be very persuasive,' Katie sighed.

Beth laughed. 'It's called nagging and it's an art she mastered long ago. She can coerce her way into anything. She just switches on that pleading look and then talks until you give up out of sheer weariness.'

Katie chuckled. 'But don't you love it?'

'Unfortunately.'

She had an early night, for the first time since she had arrived in London, and only felt a renewed onslaught of nerves when she arrived at the airport.

There was no Marcos around, and no one had tapped her on her shoulder, so she presumed that the unpleasant Jane had not arrived either.

Laura had described her to Beth, so hopefully she would be able to recognise the woman without too much difficulty.

She did. Jane was waiting in the roomy lounge upstairs reserved for the first class travellers, and Beth approached her cautiously.

'You've had your hair cut,' Jane greeted her, not bothering to stand up. 'Not trying to cultivate an impression of efficiency, by any chance?'

Beth sat down next to her and realised that her sister had not exaggerated. Jane did not like Laura. It was there in the tone of her voice and in the sharp look in her eyes.

She was a plain woman, somewhere in her mid-thirties, Beth reckoned, with close-cropped mousy brown hair, a pear-shaped figure that looked as though it would run to fat the minute one chocolate bar too many was consumed, and cold pale blue eyes.

The pale blue eyes were fixed maliciously on her now.

'How did you manage to talk your way into going on this trip with Marcos?' she asked. 'He never usually takes you anywhere with him.'

Beth shrugged and fished out a magazine from her bag. 'Maybe he's decided that my horizons need enlarging,' she suggested blandly.

Jane's thin lips compressed. 'I doubt that. You're only a secretary, after all.'

'How nice of you to remind me.'

She could tell that her composure was beginning to annoy the other woman. Perhaps Laura had not been quite so outspoken with her. Knowing her sister, she had probably taken the easier route of avoidance.

'Or maybe you talked your way into it. We all know about you.'

Beth lowered the magazine she had been about to read and looked coolly at the other woman.

'And what precisely do you know?'

Jane smiled, but her eyes were gleaming with malevolence. 'Oh, your reputation precedes you. David Ryan, for instance?'

So I was right, she thought. This was the informer.

'You were the one who told Marcos about...'

'Who else?' She smoothed her skirt, dusting a few invisible flecks from it. 'I thought it was my duty to do so. After all, it's not exactly professional to be conducting an affair with one of the directors, is it?'

'Of course not,' Beth gushed sarcastically. 'I can only thank you for the interest you've shown in the company, and in me too, because I'm sure you only had my welfare at heart.'

Jane looked at her with hatred. 'Anyway, that's put paid to any little ideas you might have had of sleeping with Marcos. I'm sure he's not the kind of man to fraternise with tarts.'

Beth took a deep breath. What she really wanted to do was jump to her feet and bring her magazine resoundingly down on Jane's head, but she had no intention of giving in to any such impulse. She knew instinctively that composure was the only way to deal with this level of dislike.

'I'm sure you're right,' she said placidly, opening the magazine and turning the pages with interest. She could feel the other woman simmering beside her, waiting for an opportunity to continue the conversation.

It was almost laughable, she thought. And of course blatantly transparent. Jane Morris had done everything in her power to blacken Laura's name, because of the little green monster.

It accounted for Marcos's insinuations that Laura was a practised temptress and Laura's own declarations that she might have joked around with some of the men in the office before David appeared on the scene, but that it had got no further than that.

She began reading one of the articles, ignoring Jane's presence, only glancing up when the Tannoy informed them that it was time to board. There was still no sign of Marcos anywhere, and Beth had a sudden, awful thought. What if he had been delayed somehow? Four days with Jane was a fate worse than death.

'I hope,' Jane said with an insincere little snicker, 'that you won't let anything I've just told you get in the way of work.'

Beth looked at her pityingly. 'Why should I? Don't you know that there's nothing you could tell me that would have an effect on me whatsoever?'

They boarded the plane in frozen silence. She was almost glad to see Marcos finally arrive. He gave her a brief smile and a nod.

'Marcos?' Jane beckoned with a saccharine smile. She patted the seat next to her. 'I've brought my papers with me; I thought we might go over some of them on the way over.'

He slid his long body next to her, and Beth continued where she had left off with her magazine, listening to their low murmur on her left with irritation.

There was a reason behind Jane's jealousy of Laura, Beth realised. It wasn't simply that Jane was painfully unglamorous, though too vain ever to see herself in that light, and Laura was not.

No, Jane was infatuated with Marcos. It was apparent in the semi-flirtatious expression she wore whenever she looked at him.

And there were a lot of those. During the nine-hour flight, Beth caught herself glancing surreptitiously at them, noticing the way Jane touched him lightly ever so often, her hand lingering on his arm as they pored over some piece of paper. Always making sure that any conversation he began with Beth was instantly diverted back to herself.

And Marcos, she was amazed to see, wasn't aware of it at all.

But then, she thought acidly, why should he be? If she was right, and his type was along the lines of Angela Fordyce, then poor Jane wouldn't enter his scope at all. He saw her strictly as a working companion and was totally oblivious to any provocation behind her movements.

She was almost tempted to tell Jane that she had nothing to fear from her. Marcos Adrino was anything but sexy as far as she was concerned.

'Enjoyed the flight?' he asked, leaning over to her, as the plane descended towards Hewanorra International Airport.

'Luxurious,' Beth averred. 'A great way to travel for my first trip abroad.'

'First trip?' Jane piped up, inclining her body so that she could see Beth more clearly. 'Surely not. And I always thought that you would be the well-travelled sort.' She said it in a tone of voice that suggested an insult, and Beth stiffened.

'I'm not,' she said shortly, thankful that the roar of the engine as the plane landed made any further conversation impossible.

'You don't mind if I grip your hand, Marcos?' she heard Jane asking. 'I'm ever so nervous about landings.' She giggled coyly. 'I have a very sensitive disposition, you know. I can be as hard as nails when I'm in the office, but this sort of thing brings out the little girl in me.'

Marcos looked faintly startled, but acquiesced politely, and Beth watched Jane's fingers curl around his brown wrist.

She felt her stomach plummet as the plane bumped over the tarmac and then braked to a halt, slowly turning until it had finally stopped, and the passengers began to stand up, stretching and reaching for their bags in the overhead lockers.

They moved swiftly through customs. Beth could see some of the other passengers, mostly women, glancing furtively across at Marcos, wondering whether they should recognise him.

And, she admitted grudgingly, he certainly had an air about him. He was dressed casually in a pair of light grey trousers and an off-white shirt carelessly rolled to the elbows. An outfit that somehow managed to do much more for him than it would have done for anyone else.

His arms were strong and sprinkled with fine dark hair, and he moved with the easy grace of someone born to be in command. Jane was clearly in her element, and Beth thought with self-disgust that she was almost as bad, staring at him as though she had never seen a member of the male sex before.

Had she forgotten that she was here to work, as he had put it in no uncertain terms? More importantly, had she forgotten that men were not conducive to peace of mind, least of all men like him?

She wondered how he could have actually listened to anything Jane had had to say about Laura, and then realised that her sister, with her flamboyantly tousled hair streaming down her back, and that vivacious glint in her eyes, didn't exactly encourage the image of a shy, reserved individual.

She grinned to herself. He must have thought he was going mad when he had been confronted with her, same green eyes, but with a far more sober expression in them, and a neat little bob.

Outside the sun was brilliant, and Beth stood still for a moment, her eyes taking in the sharp azure of the skies, the vivid green of the foliage here and there.

It was everything she had imagined, and more. There was something steamy and untamed about this tropical island.

His contact was waiting for them at the airport. He was a young man with fresh good looks and a crisp English accent. He led them to the car, chatting to Marcos about his ideas for the hotel, but it didn't escape Beth that he had shown more than just friendly interest in her.

Nor had it escaped Jane, but Beth didn't care. It felt so good to be in the warmth, her light cotton dress blowing gently around her legs, that she didn't care about anything at all.

They were staying at one of the hotels to the very north of the island, relatively close to where Marcos had earmarked the site for his own development, and Beth relaxed in the air-conditioned car, silently appreciating the scenery as they headed off.

It really was a breathtakingly beautiful island. Roger, who was driving the car, explained for her benefit bits and pieces of the island's history, pointing out the huge banana plantations as they drove through. In the rearview mirror she caught his eyes and smiled, listening in rapt silence as around them the dense, bright greenery of the plantation flashed past.

It was mountainous and lush, its hidden depths speaking to them with the noises of animals and insects.

They emerged from the hills into Castries and then further north where the houses seemed to be flattened against the hillside and framed by a wild green backdrop studded with the vivid colours of the bougainvillaea plants.

Too soon they had arrived at their hotel, a large place overlooking Reduit Bay with its white sand and shimmering water in the distance.

Beth got out of the car and stretched her legs, temporarily oblivious to everyone else as she stared around her.

Only Roger's voice at her side brought her back to reality.

'Stunning, isn't it?' he asked, his handsome, boyish face breaking into a grin.

Beth grinned back stupidly. 'And some.'

'I know you're here to work,' he said, glancing across to where Marcos was standing with Jane, involved in some discussion, 'but maybe we could get together for some drinks a bit later?'

'Maybe,' Beth said vaguely.

She could well do without the unexpected complication of Roger, however nice he was, but she knew that an outright refusal would have offended him, and anyway, what was the harm in a few drinks?

She turned towards the hotel to see Marcos looking at her through narrowed eyes. Jane shot her a triumphant glance and whispered something to him.

This, Beth thought wearily, was going to be a long four days, however splendid the scenery was.

CHAPTER FOUR

ROGER followed them into the hotel, and then told Marcos that he had set up the meeting with the various local dignitaries and Herb Brewster, the Caribbean national manager of the Adrino chain, for eight that evening.

'I don't know whether you'll need me around at this stage of the discussions?' he asked, glancing involuntarily to where Beth was standing, idly perusing some of the hotel's promotional literature.

Marcos followed the line of his gaze expressionlessly, and Beth looked up in time to see Jane smiling craftily at her.

She gave them all a large, guileless smile and Roger's grin grew broader.

She sincerely hoped that Roger would not prove to be the persistent type. She abhorred the idea of leading men on—not that there had exactly been a series of them cluttering up her life anyway.

Craig had been the only one in as long as she could remember who had managed to break through the glaring hands-off signals she gave off.

She had watched Laura's constant entourage of men with amusement, but that sort of thing was not for her, she had decided a long time ago. But Craig had persisted, growing first piqued, then bored, then angry at her refusal to sleep with him. He had eventually left, leaving her to wonder whether it had all been worth it.

Could a man never enjoy a relationship without assuming that sex would be the inevitable outcome?

Marcos was frowning slightly at her, but Roger either did not notice or else saw nothing sinister in it. He sidled across to her and whispered, 'Tonight? How about a drink? I'm staying at one of the other hotels and the bigwigs will be having their meeting. So say I pick you up here around nine o'clock?'

The question hung in the air, and out of the corner of her eye she could see Marcos looking at her, his face grim.

'Why not?' she replied on impulse. If Marcos thought the worse of her, then that was his affair. She surely wouldn't be required to do any work on her first evening in St Lucia?

As soon as Roger had left, Jane approached her and said in a voice loud enough for Marcos to hear, 'My, you do establish your... contacts quickly.'

Beth bit back the retort. 'You're quite welcome to join us.'

'I wouldn't dream of it,' Jane said loudly. 'You know what they say about two's company. Anyway, I have some homework to catch up on later. I do envy you just being a secretary. Personally speaking, I don't think I'll have the time to enjoy this lovely island.'

Shame, Beth thought to herself, you must be very stupid to pass up the opportunity of seeing this wonderful place simply in an effort to impress Marcos Adrino.

She watched as Jane left for her room with an airy wave, preceded by the porter carrying her luggage, and was about to do the same when she felt Marcos's hand close around her arm.

'Not so fast,' he drawled.

Beth stopped in her tracks and turned to face him, staring pointedly down at where he was gripping her arm. It was lost on him. He continued to grasp her, leading her across to one of the bars.

'Care for a drink?' he asked.

'No. Thank you.'

'What will it be? Something long and cold?'

Beth shrugged and tried to ignore the sensation of his fingers on her bare flesh. His hand was warm on her skin and sent a little *frisson* of awareness through her body.

'I'll have a grapefruit juice,' she said finally, realising that any attempt to get to her room was futile. This man was not accustomed to having his implicit orders countermanded, and he wasn't about to change now.

'Fine.' He ordered drinks for them both, and ushered her across to a chair.

'What do you think of St Lucia so far?' he asked, his dark eyes meeting hers directly.

Beth's gaze shifted away from him. Whenever he looked at her so intently, she immediately began to feel nervous and self-conscious.

'It's beautiful.'

'I hope it doesn't go to your head.'

'Meaning?'

'Meaning that you seem to have forgotten my little warning to you.'

'I haven't.' Why pretend that she didn't know what he was talking about?

'And it still didn't stop you from making arrangements to see Roger Drew tonight?' he asked softly.

Beth's eyes flashed. 'I didn't think that all my time here was answerable to you!'

'It is if I tell you so.'

'Don't you think that that's a little autocratic?' she asked sweetly, stifling her anger at his attitude. She had never met someone so arrogant in her life before. Was it really any wonder that she disliked him so much?

'You're not here on a goddammed holiday.'

'I realise that. And I wouldn't have made arrangements to see anyone if I knew that there was work to be done. But, unlike Jane,' she couldn't resist adding, even though she could hear the childish edge in her voice, 'I don't have a workload to take to bed.'

'So you've decided to replace it with something else? Or, should I say, someone else?'

'How dare you?'

'I dare because you work for me. A little detail that you seem to have conveniently put to the back of your mind.' He sipped from his drink, and continued to stare at her from under his long lashes.

Beth wanted to tell him that it was none of his business what she did with Roger Drew, but sensed instinctively that such a remark would be akin to playing dangerously close to a fire.

She had already come close to losing her sister's job for her. There was no point in pushing her luck.

If only, she thought. If only it were *my* job, then I'd tell him exactly what he could do with it. She tried to think of the bliss of never having to set eyes on that devilishly handsome face in her life again, but her mind refused to co-operate. Had he got so much under her skin? she wondered uneasily.

'Something about you doesn't add up,' he said lazily, not taking his eyes off her. 'I don't know if it's the impression you're trying to make, but with that new hairdo you seem to be trying to give off different signals. Now, though, I can see that it was just my mind playing tricks on me. I mean, you seem to have forgotten Ryan with the greatest of ease, don't you?'

Beth fidgeted in her chair, her face burning. She hated mention of David Ryan's name. He was the man who had betrayed her sister, and anyway, she was hardly qualified to talk about him.

But Marcos obviously expected some kind of answer.

'I haven't forgotten him,' she said, lowering her eyes.

'Trying to, then?' he prompted, his eyes hard. 'Trying to drown your lovesick blues in another man?'

'No! I'm not trying to do any such thing!'

'Then what? Don't tell me that you still feel anything for him.'

'Yes, I do!' She remembered her sister's words, her pathetic expressions of love. 'I still love him!' It was out before she could help herself, and she saw an icy shutter clamp down over his eyes.

'Love?' he scorned. 'Is that how you express your love? By leading on Drew?' He sat forward and, his action too quick to be avoidable, took her face between his hands, forcing her to look at him.

Beth had the buckling sensation of going under.

'I won't allow it!' he asserted.

'It's none of your business,' she exploded, her anger partly aimed at herself for having expressed an opinion that she was really not qualified to speak on. How could she have let this stupid charade overcome her natural sense of discretion? How could she have let slip anything about David, when, whether Marcos knew it or not, it had nothing to do with her personally?

She hated this deceit. Not for the first time, she wished desperately that she had stuck to her guns and refused to give in to her sister.

'It damned well is! Have you forgotten that he's a member of my company? Have you forgotten that I don't need my secretary to shout her indiscretions from the roof-tops?'

'I'm doing nothing of the sort!' she protested feebly. But she could see all too clearly how she must appear in his eyes. A woman who had slept with one man, in fact still professed to love him, yet was not against making a rendezvous with another the minute the opportunity arose.

There was blatant scorn on his face. It was this contempt that made her burst out vehemently, 'I don't lecture to you on how you conduct your personal life!' She held her breath, waiting for the inevitable fury, but none came.

Instead, he relaxed back in his chair. 'Would you like to?' he asked with lazy interest.

'Would I like to what?' She still felt dazed at this abrupt departure from what she had expected.

'Lecture to me on my personal life. I know you've got a bagful of opinions on it, even though it's clear to the both of us that you have no right. So come on, tell me what you think. No one ever has before. It might make an amusing change.'

There was silence. Was this yet another game he was playing with her? she wondered. He seemed to be waiting for her answer, mildly curious, his long fingers stroking the side of his glass absent-mindedly.

'I really don't think that we ought to be having this conversation,' she ventured awkwardly. 'I am only your secretary, after all.'

'You mean if we had slept together, you might have had more of a right to tell me what you thought?'

His voice was tantalisingly soft and it sent an excited shiver through her.

Unbidden, a thousand thoughts sprang into her head. Slept with him. If she had slept with him. What would it be like?

She suddenly felt so strong a yearning to find out that she gasped in shock.

Those long, clever fingers, what would it be like to feel them exploring her body, to feel his mouth moving restlessly against hers?

My God, she thought with a flood of panic, get a grip on yourself! You've been disillusioned once before, remember? He's not your type, remember?

'It's not my place to volunteer any information like that,' she whispered huskily, not daring to look at him fully in the face, concentrating on the potted plant just to the right of him. A magnificent dwarf palm that would never have survived in England.

'It's not stopped you before. In fact, until recently, I assumed that you didn't have any opinions on my private life one way or another, but now—well, tell me. It's an order.'

'If you really want to know,' Beth began hesitatingly, her body rigid with tension, 'from what I've seen, you don't mind using women for your own ends. You take them and, as soon as they stop amusing you, you have no qualms in dropping them. Like a child that suddenly loses interest in a plaything. Don't you care that they might be more involved with you than you are with them?'

She thought of Angela Fordyce, desperate enough to accost him in his office even though he had finished with her. She looked like a woman who had always pulled the strings, except with Marcos.

'Why do you object to that? Aren't you the same?'

Beth's automatic response was to deny the accusation, but how could she?

'Besides,' he continued when she remained silent, 'I never give promises I can't keep. True enough, I wine, dine and bed them, but I play fairly. I never let them think that the relationship stretches beyond those parameters.'

'You make sure that they don't get their feet into the front door.'

'That's right,' he drawled. 'I never was interested in playing house—not as a little boy, and not now. Marriage is one institution I don't intend to succumb to. From what I've seen, the attractions are invariably short-lived.'

Beth swallowed some of the fruit juice. She felt as though they were entirely alone, swept up into some terribly intimate vortex.

'I see,' she said.

'I'm sure you do.' The knowing criticism behind his words snapped her back to reality.

For a second she had an insane desire to confess everything to him, but of course it was insane. She was in too deep now to fall victim to any such impulse.

All she could do was ride with the tide and hope that it brought her to safe shores eventually.

'What time do we start work tomorrow?' she asked, her voice still unsteady. She had to bring this conversation back to a manageable level. At all costs.

Marcos shot her a lazy, assessing look. 'Nine. I have a meeting with some planners. I'll want you there to take notes and you can type up the necessary report in the afternoon. I've instructed the hotel to have a typewriter installed in your bedroom. Not as advanced as the computer, but it'll have to do.'

'Certainly.' Her voice was definitely more controlled now. She risked a glance at him and felt another strange quiver shoot through her.

'I think I'll leave now,' she muttered, standing up, eager to escape his company. 'I need a bath, and I have unpacking to do...' Her voice tapered out.

'Have a nice night out. With Roger. And take this as a warning: keep your hands off him. You can bed-hop with anyone else, just so long as he doesn't work for me.'

He meant it too. Every word. The threat lay there in those black eyes and in the grim lines of his mouth.

Beth walked away quickly, her heart beating so loudly that it hurt. She barely noticed her surroundings as she followed the porter to her bedroom, anxious for him to leave so that she could release her body from its heightened tension in privacy.

As soon as he had gone, she felt herself go limp. She ran a bath, settling comfortably into it and wished that her thoughts were as comfortable.

But they weren't. They were chaotic, mad, teasing little shadows that fluttered away the minute she tried to control them.

If only she could stand back from Marcos, but something inside her refused to oblige. She felt like a moth, lured by a bright light, but bright lights, she reminded herself, could be fatal to unsuspecting moths.

She had a light supper in her room, excusing herself to Jane on the weak grounds that she wanted to get some rest before she went out that evening.

'Fine,' Jane agreed coolly, 'as I told you, I have a lot of reading to do anyway. Where are you and Roger going?' There was a tinge of envy in her voice which

Beth ignored. She felt sorry for Jane. The other woman was obviously lonely and loneliness often bred spite.

'I don't know,' Beth said pleasantly. 'We'll probably just stay here for a drink. I want an early night.'

'Really?' She said that in a tone that implied disbelief. 'Well, have a good time.'

'Thank you,' Beth replied politely.

Actually the last thing she needed was an evening of stilted conversation with someone she didn't know from Adam, but it would have been churlish to have now given him some excuse, having promised earlier to meet him.

She had a quick nap, and then dressed hurriedly in a pair of lilac culottes and a matching flowered blouse.

Roger was waiting downstairs for her. He ran his eyes approvingly over her slim body and ushered her out to where the car was waiting.

'But I thought we could stay here,' Beth protested.

'I know a nice little place. Much cosier than here.' He smiled warmly at her. 'Don't worry about my keeping you out too late. I have orders to collect the master at a specific time.'

'The master?' She giggled, relaxing. 'Is that how you refer to Marcos?'

Roger grinned at her, opening the car door for her to enter. 'Don't you think that it's an apt description?'

'It has a ring about it,' she agreed, staring out of the window as the car pulled out of the confines of the hotel.

She had rolled the window down, and the sultry breeze blew lazily over her, whipping her hair around her face.

The darkness around them was alive with night sounds, the peaceful calling of insects. It filled the air, a constant reminder that there, in the shadows, life on a different level was throbbing and alive.

They drove to a charming bar, all verandas and gables, and Beth happily allowed Roger to lead the conversation for the evening, relishing the warmth and enjoying his amusing anecdotes.

She liked Roger. He was relaxing. Nothing about him taxed her, or set her on edge. In fact, he was as diametrically opposed to Marcos as anyone could be.

She had two piña coladas, and found that she was laughing a lot and really rather enjoying herself.

'Can we do this again?' Roger asked when they were back at the hotel.

'Who knows?' Beth replied evasively. 'It was fun, but I have an awful lot of work to get through while I'm here.' And besides, she added to herself, Marcos is watching me, and for some ridiculous reason I care what he thinks.

'Is that a polite brush-off?' His voice was lightheartedly resigned rather than mortally offended, and for that she was glad.

'I don't want involvement,' she said truthfully.

'Does that just apply to me, or is the rest of the male species included?'

'Oh, the latter.' She laughed, and had another, unexpectedly vivid image of Marcos's cynical face, then she blinked and the vision vanished.

'Why not?'

'I like my life the way it is at the moment,' she responded, hearing a shade of doubt in her voice. She always had liked the simplicity of her life, its untroubled predictability. Craig had temporarily ruffled the calm surface, but afterwards the ripples had gradually smoothed over and things had returned to what they had been. She had seen it as a salutary experience. So why was she beginning to feel dissatisfied now?

'So we part as platonic friends?' Roger asked lightly, and she nodded. 'Platonic friends can still have drinks together, you know. Or do you have a rule against that as well?'

'No rule.'

'Then if the opportunity arises?'

'Sure. A platonic drink would be very enjoyable.' They smiled at one another, and then he bent forwards, brushing his lips against hers, deepening his kiss until she pulled away.

'That,' he informed her ruefully, 'was just my way of saying goodbye to what might have been. And now I'll leave you in peace. The Prince of Darkness summons.' They laughed, and Beth made her way back to the bedroom. The two piña coladas had made her feel pleasantly fuzzy, and Roger's company had been a welcome change from the confused tension which she always felt in Marcos's presence.

Not, she thought the following morning, that there was an opportunity to feel anything except exhausted. The meeting was hard, and she sat alongside Marcos, barely finding the time to look up, her hand flying over her pad as she took notes of everything that was being said. Jane made sure that she contributed her fair share to what was being discussed, glancing across every so often at Beth, reminding her of their different responsibilities.

'There's no need to lock yourself away and type all this up,' Marcos told her, as the meeting dispersed. 'It seems a shame to waste this weather. Why don't you go down to the beach?'

Jane had edged towards them. She fluttered her lashes in Marcos's direction. 'I will, even if Beth doesn't,' she said. 'I need a tan, don't you think? Are you coming down? I'd feel much safer with a man around. The sea can be a scary place to a city gal like me.'

'I hardly think there's anything to fear if you stay close to the shore,' he said drily, glancing at her.

Beth could almost feel Jane vibrating under his dark gaze.

'Get your swimsuit,' he told Beth, turning to face her, and she replied tartly,

'Is that another order?'

'You're beginning to catch on.'

Jane was watching this interchange suspiciously. 'Perhaps Roger would like to tag along?' she interjected. 'By the way, did you have a good time last night?'

Marcos's expression changed imperceptibly. 'Drew's tied up for the whole of today,' he informed Beth, his voice hard.

'What a shame,' a little stab of mischief prompted her to reply. 'And yes,' she added, looking at Jane, 'we had a lovely time last night.'

Marcos's face grew grimmer. 'I'll see you two on the beach in ten minutes. We can have lunch there.'

'Promise?' Jane's lips pouted, but Marcos wasn't looking at her at all. He was looking at Beth, his eyes silently reminding her of his warning, and she smiled innocently back at him.

She refused to be daunted on a day like this. When the sky was so perfectly blue, and in the distance she could see the silvery sparkle of the water, crystal-clear and invitingly warm.

'I'll see you both on the beach, then,' she affirmed cheerily, and pranced back to the bedroom, dumping her stack of notes on the bed, and quickly changing into her swimming costume.

It really was a minuscule affair. Jade-green and designed to attract attention. Typical of her sister.

She modestly covered herself with a loose-fitting T-shirt, but the minute she removed it she realised exactly how revealing the bikini was by the heads that swivelled around as she walked past.

Jane's mouth fell open, but it was Marcos's reaction which made her face turn red. He was staring at her through narrowed eyes, and she felt suddenly and powerfully aware of just how much of her breasts was exposed.

Jane looked at them both and broke the silence. 'The sea looks great, doesn't it, Marcos?' It worked. His attention reluctantly shifted away from Beth and he began chatting to Jane.

Beth took the opportunity to stretch out her beach towel, a little distance away from theirs, and she lay down on it, diligently applying the suntan oil over her body.

Nevertheless she was frighteningly aware of Marcos next to her, his body lean and mesmerising, clad only in his swimming trunks. He certainly didn't look as though he needed a tan at all. It wasn't fair. Couldn't he have one little bit of physical imperfection?

Even relaxing as he was now, there was something aggressive about him. Maybe it had something to do with his physique. It struck her forcibly just how devastatingly attractive he was and she stopped herself before she was besieged by any more unwelcome thoughts.

Instead, she looked around her. Reduit Beach was most people's idea of paradise. It stretched away into the distance, a seemingly never-ending expanse of soft white sand leading down to turquoise waters.

It was fairly uncrowded, freckled with holiday makers, some of whom looked as though they were applying the same precision to their tanning as they would have done to their jobs. Half an hour on the front, half an hour on the back, a quick dip in the sea, then starting all over again.

Laura would have loved this, Beth thought wistfully. Neither of them had ever travelled very much. There had simply not been enough money to stretch to such luxuries when they were growing up. Their holidays had mostly been spent at beaches in England, and there was no comparison.

Jane had managed to persuade Marcos to accompany her into the sea, and Beth idly watched as their figures were swallowed by the water.

Marcos immediately began swimming out to sea, his strokes strong and assured, while Jane paddled about close to the shore and hungrily followed his progress.

When he was safely in the distance, Beth made her way to the water, submerging herself, her body temperature adjusting remarkably quickly to the temperature of the water. She made desultory conversation with Jane, finding her continual barbed comments more of an irritation than an insult, and when she could stand no more she began swimming out.

It was wonderfully liberating being surrounded only by water, water so clear that she could easily see down to the sandy bottom.

She was about to begin the haul back to shore when a sudden pain shot through her calf and she yelped in agony, spluttering as she frantically made an effort to keep above the surface of the water.

She could barely move her leg and she floundered, desperately trying to massage it back into life while not drowning in the process.

Of course she wouldn't drown; she had only to holler for help. Nevertheless, she was relieved when she felt arms around her, supporting her body at the waist.

'Thanks,' she murmured sheepishly, twisting to see her rescuer, then the smile froze on her lips.

Why Marcos? Why, when there were other people in the water, did it have to be Marcos who was now helping her back to land, his arms sending prickles of heat through her?

'What happened?' Jane asked, only to be abruptly told by Marcos that there was no need for her to accompany them.

'Cramp,' Beth explained and Jane's mouth tightened.

He helped her back to her towel and sat her down gently.

'Suffer often with this?' he asked, squatting next to her. He began kneading her foot and Beth instinctively pulled away. 'Don't act like a child,' he said tersely. She relaxed reluctantly, letting him massage her calf, the rhythmic movements of his hands gradually easing the painful knot.

'It's fine now,' she said, as soon as she possibly could. She flexed her ankle tentatively, then with more confidence as the pain faded. 'I'm all right.'

'Don't I deserve a thank-you?'

'Thank you,' she murmured obediently, wishing that he would vanish back into the water and leave her alone.

She lay down flat on the towel and squinted against the sun, but was uncomfortably aware that he had not budged.

'There's no need for you to baby-sit me, you know,' she hinted.

'I'm not.'

'Then why don't you go back into the water?' she asked, abandoning any pretence of subtlety.

'Because the view from here is infinitely more satisfying,' he said. He leaned over her so that he blocked out the sun and the warmth in his eyes made the blood rush madly to her head.

She couldn't think straight. She couldn't even seem to move her limbs because a strange torpor had settled over them, and they felt like lead weights.

'I don't think I've ever seen quite such a small bikini before,' he murmured. 'I can't imagine why you don't dispense with it altogether.'

Laura, she thought desperately, this is your fault. My modest one-piece is languishing back in Cambridge and here I am, decked out in this tiny green thing that leaves nothing to the imagination.

There was no response to that remark, none that she could think of anyway. She smiled weakly and hoped that he couldn't hear the thudding of her heart under her ribcage.

'I don't appear to have noticed before,' he was saying, his eyes straying over her body, 'but you really are remarkably attractive. But you know that already, don't you?'

'Do I?' Beth squeaked.

'No one who wears a bikini like that is unaware of the effect she has on men.'

It's not my bikini, she wanted to wail. His observations were a curious blend of perceptiveness and misjudgements, as though he could see into her depths but was constantly being fooled by surface appearance. Hardly surprising when she was masquerading under a false identity.

'Isn't it nearly time for lunch?' she questioned in a feeble attempt to change the conversation.

He was not to be so easily diverted.

'In fact, right now, I could be sorely tempted to break my own rules about non-involvement between members of staff.'

Beth's body froze as she felt his finger trail a path along her collarbone, down to the inviting valley between her breasts, which were aching as though in anticipation of forbidden delights.

She wondered where Jane was. Still obeying orders and splashing about in the water?

She could hardly breathe. His finger finished its delicate exploration of her cleavage, then moved up the swell of her breast until she felt it circle the hardened tip of her nipple, rubbing it gently till she was drowning under a barrage of new and overpowering sensations.

She had never been touched by a man before, not like this. Marcos made her whole body pulse with response, electrified her until she was filled with a need that frightened her with its intensity.

'Please,' she uttered, 'no.'

'You don't like it?' His voice was rough and as unsteady as her own. He moved his finger to her other waiting nipple, and it swelled under his touch.

'Does Ryan make you feel like this?'

Beth's half-closed eyes shot open, and her brain cleared instantly. What the hell was she doing? Had she completely taken leave of her senses?

She sat up and pulled her T-shirt over her.

'Get away from me,' she said numbly.

'Why? Don't tell me that your thoughts were on Ryan, because I won't believe you. Can you really try and convince me that you love another man when I can feel you opening up under my fingers like a flower?'

'I don't have to tell you anything at all.'

'And you don't object to whatever conclusions I draw?' he asked tightly.

'Please, just leave me alone.'

'My pleasure.' The contempt was back in his eyes as he looked at her and she wanted the ground to open up and swallow her.

She was still trembling when he walked away.

CHAPTER FIVE

BETH was hardly aware of what they ate for lunch. She knew from the menu that it was typical local fare—crabback with cheesy christophene and salad—and normally she would have savoured every mouthful, but it tasted like cardboard.

She couldn't even summon up the energy to respond to Jane's slyly caustic comments, although she was aware of the other girl watching her suspiciously out of the corner of her eye.

She was still too shocked by what had happened on the beach. Marcos had touched her and all of a sudden her world had shifted on its axis. Her careful, neat little arrangement of emotions had been shattered, and what had been exposed was a primitive yearning that she had not even known she possessed. Nothing she had felt for Craig had prepared her for this.

The sheer force of it had knocked her for six.

Around her, Marcos and Jane conversed politely, and she joined in when it was necessary, her mouth finding the right responses though her mind was miles away.

What a fool she had been. What a silly, gullible little fool.

Marcos didn't look as though he had been in the slightest bit affected by what had happened between them. But then, she thought bitterly, why should he? He had only, after all, used her to satisfy his curiosity. For a while, she had turned him on, and he had reacted. The fact that she had responded to him only proved his point that she had no scruples.

She had never before in her life felt so helpless.

She was relieved when he politely excused himself, saying that he had an appointment to view his potential site. She barely noticed that Jane had remained where she was, sipping her fruit juice, until she spoke.

'How's your leg feeling?'

Beth looked at her warily. It was an inoffensive enough question, but she knew from experience that very few of Jane's remarks to her were ever devoid of some undertone of malice.

'Much better, thank you.'

'I suppose you think you're clever, don't you?' she asked conversationally, rolling her glass in between her fingers so that the ice cubes clinked together.

'I have no idea what you're talking about.' Beth glanced at her. Her face was beginning to show the hallmarks of too much sun. Her nose was tinged red, as were her cheeks, and her hair, without the aid of a brush as they had lunched straight from the beach, hung in short, uneven strands around her face. She was wearing a white T-shirt, an unflattering colour on her without the benefit of a tan.

Beth sighed. Right now, she just wasn't up to a bout of verbal warfare, but she had a feeling that that was just what she was in for.

'Don't think that I didn't see through that phoney cramp routine,' she bit out without preamble.

'It wasn't phoney!'

She carried on as though Beth had not spoken. 'Don't think that I don't know that you'd do anything to get Marcos's attention.'

'And how was I supposed to know that he would be the one to come to my aid?' Beth enquired logically, holding on to her calm with great difficulty. 'Believe it or not, I don't have eyes in the back of my head!'

As a matter of fact, he was the last person she had wanted around, but she wasn't going to say that.

'Look,' she said wearily, 'can't we stop all this and at least be civil towards one another? I have no axe to grind with you, and we are going to be here for another two days. We could at least call a temporary truce.' She ventured a smile but met with no response.

'I would if I could see anything likeable about you. Ever since you joined the company, you've rubbed me up the wrong way. Preening and posing and acting as though you're God's gift to men.'

Had Laura acted like that? Beth doubted it. Her sister was vivacious and bubbly, like a glass of champagne, but she was not the kind of girl ever to court disfavour with anyone, and she certainly didn't preen and pose.

'I think that remark is totally uncalled for,' she snapped.

'I don't care what you think! I can only repeat what I've said before. You're wasting your time with Marcos. Men like him don't need women like you. They can have anyone they want. Do you really think that he would find anything about you appealing?'

'You're wasting your time, and mine, Jane. I'm not interested in him.'

'Doesn't look that way to me.'

Her eyes were chips of ice in a face distorted by anger.

'In case you didn't know, inter-company relationships are strictly forbidden...' Beth began appeasingly.

'Not that you would ever let that stand in your way.'

There was a heavy silence and Beth wondered what she could say to pour oil on these waters. Nothing, she decided. She had no reason to justify herself.

At the back of her mind, though, a little nagging thought began to spout. What if, without wanting it, she was attracted to Marcos? Of course she couldn't be, but then again, she had reacted to him in a way that was totally uncharacteristic and uncontrolled.

Maybe Jane had picked up her unconscious response. And if Jane had picked it up, who was to say that Marcos hadn't as well?

The thought made her go cold.

'Why do you care what I think of Marcos anyway?' she asked eventually.

Jane reddened.

'Look,' Beth said, feeling a surge of pity for the other woman, 'he goes in for beautiful blondes. You're right. He's a man who can pick and choose, and those are the types he chooses. Surely there are lots of men out there; you're not unattractive...' Her voice faltered as the embarrassment on Jane's face gave way to fury.

Too late, Beth realised that she had chosen the wrong words to express her sympathy. Jane would not want to be told that Marcos was as out of her reach as a shooting star.

'This is silly,' she began, hastily trying to retrace her steps. 'Marcos is not interested in either of us...'

Oh, lord, she groaned inwardly. How much more tactless can I get?

'Don't patronise me,' Jane hissed furiously. 'I may not be tall and blonde——'

'I didn't mean it in that——'

'—but I know one thing for sure. If I can't have Marcos, then you certainly won't!'

She stood up and swept away, her head held high.

Beth remained where she was, ordering a cup of tea, even though the weather was so hot, thoughtfully taking small sips out of it. Tea was a great soother, a lovely British habit that never failed her.

What a mess, she thought. Not only had Marcos Adrino shown her that she was far more of a vulnerable fool than she had ever suspected, but from the look of it he had managed to turn Jane's world upside-down as well. How long had the poor woman been nurturing her dreams? Had her obsession with him crept up on her insidiously, like some dreadful illness, only becoming apparent when it was too late to take preventative measures?

Men like him, she thought angrily, ought to have a health warning on them. It was at least a small blessing that Laura had remained untouched by his charm. She preferred the adoring kind of man, and Beth somehow could never see Marcos in that role.

No, he had been brutally honest with her when he had told her that commitment was not for him. He preferred the excitement of the chase, the sweet short period of possession, and then the freedom to discard.

If I had read his character reference on paper, Beth decided, I would have disliked him on the spot.

She wandered up to her room for a short siesta and gloomily contemplated the remainder of the day.

They were due to accompany him on a sightseeing tour of the island, to get the feel of the community, he had told them earlier on. Just the three of them. It had the makings of a nightmare.

Outside the sun poured through the window. She could imagine the sizzling heat, even though it was beautifully cool inside the bedroom with the air-conditioning on.

She tried to doze, but every time she felt herself sinking into sleep some new disturbing thought would flash through her mind, and finally she gave up altogether.

On top of everything else, she thought, that damned man has succeeded in throwing my sleeping pattern out of joint. If I develop insomnia I'll damn well charge the sleeping tablets to his account.

Poor Jane, she thought sympathetically, at least he only invades my thoughts because I dislike him. Imagine how awful to be infatuated with him, to be haunted by his image, like something tauntingly close and yet inaccessible. Despite the madness of her response to him on the beach, it at least had the saving grace of only being a hiccup in her self-control, and one which would not recur.

At three o'clock she got dressed, putting on a pair of green culottes and a tan sleeveless shirt. He was waiting for her in the foyer, staring outside, half turned away, and she took the opportunity to look at him with unashamed openness.

His strong hands were thrust into the pockets of his shorts, and even thinking himself unobserved he still had something watchful and alert about him. What was going on in that mind of his? He had obviously just had a shower. His hair was still damp and was combed away from his face, emphasising the hard, ruthless stamp of his features.

He turned suddenly, catching her observation, and his expression changed to one of amusement.

Beth pursed her lips and walked towards him.

'Where's Jane?' she asked, looking around for the other girl.

'She's not coming,' Marcos responded flatly, 'something about a headache.'

'A headache?' Beth looked at him, dismay clouding her face. Simple arithmetic meant that that left only the two of them on this marvellous sightseeing tour. 'Couldn't she have taken a couple of aspirin? Doesn't she know that the fresh air will do her good?' Doesn't she know that she just can't leave me stranded like this? Her prickly nature might be irritating, but it was nothing compared to what Marcos aroused in her.

He shrugged indolently. 'It appears not. Why are you so concerned? I didn't sense that there was a great deal of love lost between the two of you.'

He began walking out of the foyer towards the car and Beth followed helplessly, half running to keep up with him.

Once outside the confines of the hotel, with its central air-conditioning system, the heat wrapped around her lovingly. There was enough of a breeze to temper the warmth and she tossed her hair back.

'Perhaps she's feeling a bit better,' she offered hopefully, as he unlocked her car door.

'Perhaps,' Marcos replied drily, 'you're scared of being alone with me.'

Beth jumped into the car and slammed the door behind her.

'Well?' he prompted softly as the car throbbed into life. 'Have I hit the nail on the head?'

'Certainly not!' she denied hotly, but as he drove out he was whistling, as though the thought was affording him a great deal of amusement.

'So tell me something about yourself,' he said, driving fairly slowly over the bumpy road. He shot her a swift glance and grinned.

'You're in a sparkling mood,' Beth muttered.

'I guess I am. Things are going well with the project.'

'They are?' She relaxed a bit as curiosity got the better of her. That, and the fact that Marcos Adrino could be disarmingly charming at times. 'Did you look around the site?'

'I did, and it's just what I had in mind. Close to the sea, but without any other hotels nudging it from the sides. And an untamed, lush backdrop that looks as though it's stepped straight out of a postcard.'

'The sort of place that encourages people to lose track of time?' Beth volunteered, her mind captivated by the image.

Marcos darted her another appraising look. 'Precisely. You have a knack with words, has anyone ever told you that?'

Beth laughed. 'No one that I can remember offhand.'

They were driving through dense landscape now, a carpet of banana trees, their wide leaves dancing in the breeze. Marcos pointed out a turning to Marigot Bay and Hurricane Hole, a smooth sheet of water where yachts bobbed gracefully on the currents.

Beth watched, fascinated, listening to his descriptions and immersed in the splendid scenery. It was like driving through a rain forest. She had never before seen such an abundance of flora and fauna, and then suddenly the view became dominated by the startling sight of the Pitons, twin peaks, soaring proudly upwards.

She gasped in pleasure.

'Stunning, isn't it?' Marcos said, appreciating her response. 'You should see them from the sea. Quite amazing. The sort of unforgettable sight that lives in your imagination long after you've left the island.'

'You sound quite poetic,' she teased.

'It's easy to be poetic about nature,' Marcos said semi-seriously, 'it's only slightly more difficult when you try to apply it to the human race.'

Beth looked at him, startled. 'Surely you don't believe that!'

'When you live in the concrete jungle, you see enough deception to jaundice any finer emotions you might have for the rest of your life.'

He began talking about where they were going, down towards Soufrière, the small town that lent its name to the Soufrière volcano, and Beth was relieved that the subject had been changed.

Any talk of deception was a bit too close to the bone for her liking. She suddenly pictured how Marcos would react to the deception being perpetrated on his own doorstep, and she felt her blood run cold.

He would not be amused. He certainly would not wave it aside as a childish prank. She found that she was per-spiring slightly, and focused her attention on the scenery, losing herself temporarily in it.

The Soufrière volcano, Marcos assured her, had not seen activity since the eighteenth century.

'Oh, good,' Beth said with a grin, 'it's nice to know that we're not being suicidal in coming here.'

He laughed and together they looked at the sunken crater in silence, a dead grey pool that seemed curiously lifeless amid the fertile growth.

'Back north?' he asked, and she nodded, surprised at the length of time that had elapsed. And not a moment's discomfort with him. When they hadn't been absorbed in the panoramic view, they had amicably chatted about any and everything. He had a dry sense of humour and appeared to be able to talk on any subject with ease. He seemed to know as much about music and the theatre as he did about the financial market and the economy.

'You never answered my original question,' he reminded her, as they retraced their tracks in the car, only now driving with dusk fast on their heels, instead of in blistering sunshine.

'What original question?' Beth asked, puzzled.

'The one about yourself.'

'Oh, that one. Not much to answer. I have a sister, a mother, a stepfather and no pets.'

He grinned, and the twilight lent his face a magnetic sensuality. Beth slapped down her reaction and told herself that, however pleasant he could be, he was still dangerous. It wouldn't do to let that slip her mind even for a moment.

'Sounds about right,' he murmured, driving more carefully now as the light faded.

'You have a sister, a mother, a stepfather and no pets as well?' she asked with interest, just in case he began quizzing her on Laura.

'No,' Marcos said evenly, the humour no longer apparent in his voice. 'I have none of those. My mother died when I was three and my father followed suit ten years later. He died bankrupt.'

'I'm sorry.' And she was, instinctively so. She wanted to reach out and touch him, but that was impossible. She twined her fingers together uselessly on her lap.

'Are you? So am I. I watched my father die, and I can tell you that bankruptcy is not very dignified. It's degrading and it's pathetic, especially to a man as fiercely proud as my father was.' He could not conceal his bitterness, and, as though disliking the turn in the conversation, abruptly switched the topic.

But his remarks, surely unintentional, had shown Beth a side to him that she would never have known existed. Not, she admitted, that she had given a great deal of thought to his parents and whether they were still alive, or what they did for a living.

Was that why he had had the ruthless drive to make himself a fortune? Children, she knew, often felt the compulsion to avoid the errors of their parents. She had been lucky. Her parents had had a warm and happy marriage, and she and Laura had grown up with the comforting thought that nothing was impossible.

Maybe, she thought wryly, that was why she was in this situation now.

He was talking to her about a party being given the next evening, their last evening on the island.

'A few of the local people and members of staff who have been helping with this project.'

'Where?' Beth asked.

'One of the bars in the hotel. We've rented it for the night. Should be right up your alley.'

'Meaning?'

'Don't you like dancing?'

'Oh.' Beth blushed. She had assumed the worst behind his statement. 'I suppose so, yes. Though I haven't done any of that for quite a while.'

'Now isn't that curious?' Marcos said, as the car slotted neatly into one of the vacant spaces in the hotel car park. He switched off the engine and stared at her. 'From what I gathered, you did a lot of that with Ryan.'

Beth floundered for words, finally managing to say stiltedly, 'Yes, of course. I guess I thought you were referring to the singles scene.'

Didn't that just go to prove it? she thought, angry with herself. It was too damned easy to let her guard fall when Marcos turned on the charm. When he was snarling, she made sure that all her defences were properly in place, but when he smiled she forgot all about her sense of caution, and that was a sure way to court disaster.

And he had smiled too much this afternoon for her own good. She realised that she had found herself liking him. Liking him! The thought made her suddenly uneasy, and she snapped open her door, frantic now to escape his presence.

'I'm out tonight,' he said, catching up with her easily. 'But do you fancy a drink now?'

'No,' she replied sharply, 'I mean, no, thank you. I...I think I'll pop in and make sure that Jane's all right.'

'Of course,' Marcos drawled laconically, sensing her change of mood. 'I forgot that Jane's welfare is close to your heart.'

He looked down at her, his hair tousled from the drive, and she felt a pulse begin to beat steadily in her temple.

She felt... What did she feel? My God, I want him to touch me. The yearning was so powerful that she wanted to faint from it.

She spun around on her heels and without a backward glance dashed towards the sanctuary of her bedroom, only releasing a long breath once she was inside.

As an afterthought, she dialled through to Jane's room and a drowsy voice answered.

'I just wanted to find out how you were feeling,' Beth said. She couldn't say why she was bothering to be a good Samaritan, when the girl had had nothing pleasant to say to her from day one.

'Much better, thank you.' Jane's voice sank a few degrees cooler as soon as she recognised the person at the other end, and Beth sighed. 'How was your afternoon with Marcos?'

'St Lucia is beautiful,' she replied, skirting around the question. 'We drove south towards Soufrière and then came back. It's a great place to build a hotel.'

'I don't suppose either of you even missed my company.' Jane's voice was sullen and short-tempered and Beth could well imagine the downturned mouth.

'More than you think,' she answered honestly. Face it, if Jane had been there, she would not be going through this turmoil because she would still have been cocooned in her convenient line of thinking that Marcos was an arrogant bastard.

'Oh, yes,' Jane taunted down the line, 'like a hole in the head.'

'Look,' Beth said, her patience wearing thin, 'I didn't telephone you to argue.'

'No, you telephoned me because you felt sorry for me.'

'Yes. No! What I mean is...'

'I know what you mean! Thanks for the concern, but no, thanks.'

There was the dead tone as the receiver was replaced and Beth scowled at it. Poor Laura. Little wonder that she had hoped that Jane had been eaten by her workload.

She knew that she had infinitely more patience than her sister, and when it came to Jane even her supply was wearing at the edges.

And it was non-existent in the case of Marcos. He could antagonise her beyond endurance. But, a little voice whispered, he can also make you laugh more than anyone else ever has. She ignored the little voice.

But she was extra-careful now. Throughout the following day, she kept a low profile, sheltering behind

Jane, grateful for her presence even though it could be trying most of the time.

In the afternoon, they visited the marketplace in Castries, an enchanting scene, bustling with people and jammed with all sorts of things for sale, from straw hats and bags to vegetables.

Beth conveniently detached herself from Jane and Marcos, and strolled around it at leisure, buying a couple of souvenirs to take back for Laura.

By the time they were back in the hotel, she was exhausted from the sun and the walking. The heat, she found, sapped her energy and left her ready for bed at a surprisingly early hour.

Maybe, she thought optimistically, she could creep away from the party without anyone noticing and catch up on her sleep.

And if she couldn't, then at least Roger was going to be there. She could relax with him and with any luck avoid Marcos completely. Because she had found, much to her annoyance, that her eyes still insisted on sneaking to observe him, even though her brain was firmly against any such temptation.

She dressed carefully for the party. Her sister's choice in evening wear was as flamboyant as her choice in swimsuits. If only she had thought ahead, she would have brought some of her own modest clothes down from Cambridge, but she had brought only a few working clothes and her jeans and jumpers. How was she to know that within a few days of working there she would be asked to go to St Lucia?

The black jersey dress which she chose was flattering, but extrovertly so. It was cut off the shoulder, following the curve of her breasts lovingly, falling from her waist in rich folds to mid-calf.

She applied a minimum of make-up and brushed her hair until it gleamed. Then she waited until she was perfectly sure that everyone else had arrived.

She was not into making grand entrances, and she certainly didn't intend to start now.

She knew, without conceit, that she was attractive, but she had always been more than happy to play it down, preferring to look cool and sensible rather than sexy. Her sister, with those long rippling locks and extravagant gestures, was sexy. And Beth had always chosen the other route.

She wondered whether it was because they were identical twins. Their mother had never dressed them in the same clothes, and they had been encouraged to assert their individuality from an early age.

She could remember, quite clearly, when they were only children, going to a birthday party with Laura. The hostess had exclaimed to her father how different they were, even though they looked exactly alike, feature for feature. Her father had pulled Beth on to his lap and laughed.

'This one,' he had said, tapping her nose affectionately, 'is my practical, serious little baby. Quite different from her sister, but still two sides of the same coin.'

I miss my father, she thought. The previous day, when they had been sightseeing, during one of the comfortable lulls between them, Marcos had asked her about her parents, and she had found herself confiding in him, talking about her father, saying things that had surprised her. He had managed to stir up a nest of bittersweet memories inside her.

The man, she thought now, regarding her reflection sombrely, had a talent for drawing people out, hearing their confidences. The sign of the inveterate charmer.

The man who listened was halfway to winning a woman's heart.

It was just a good job that she was clever enough to spot the danger. Not that he had any interest in winning her heart. Oh, no. That sort of thing came naturally to him. He could bowl a woman over while remaining immune to the situation.

The room was already crowded by the time she finally made it down.

There were the local people, some four or five in total, who had also brought their other halves. One had brought his two teenage daughters who wore on their pretty olive-skinned faces a mixture of shyness and delight. Then there were the company members, including Roger. He spotted her immediately and waved, moving over to take her by her arm.

'You might be late,' he informed her wolfishly, 'but you're well worth the wait.'

Beth laughed, accepting the drink that he had brought over to her, her eyes involuntarily skirting around the room, settling briefly on Marcos until she felt that familiar quickening of her pulses. Then she looked away.

He was talking to two men, dominating the conversation, while Jane hovered on the sidelines, nodding vigorously to everything he said.

He had not even seen her enter the room, and for that she was grateful. Better to be ignored than confronted by him.

She began chatting to Roger, telling him about what she had seen of the island, genuinely envious when he told her that he would be there for at least another week.

'Doing all the groundwork. The Prince of Darkness has no qualms about delegation, and actually I don't mind, because I know that he could do it all himself if

he had the time or really wanted to. That's the difference
between a good boss and a bad one. The bad ones give
orders but half the time they don't know what they're
talking about.'

'Very philosophical.' Beth grinned. 'Sounds as if the
Prince of Darkness has a fan club in you.'

Roger shrugged. 'He's bloody clever, and he's fair.
He's had to work his way up from nothing, you know.'

'I know.'

Roger looked at her in surprise. 'You know? He told
you?'

She nodded and he whistled under his breath. 'I only
know that on hearsay. From what I gather, the great
man never discusses anything personal, with anyone.
How on earth did you manage to get on his list of
confidantes?'

'I'm not!' Beth protested, her face pink. But
throughout the meal she knew that her admission had
given him food for speculation. She had connived to sit
as far away from Marcos as she feasibly could, in between Roger and a charming St Lucian gentleman, the
father of the teenage girls. Nevertheless, it was impossible to miss the strains of his deep voice. Whatever
was being discussed at that end of the table, it was obvious that he controlled it. As he seemed to do with
everything else.

As the dessert dishes were being cleared away, she
glanced across at him and for a minute their eyes locked.
He looked quickly at Roger and then back to her, and
this time there was a shade of mockery in his expression.

Beth hurriedly diverted her attention to the St Lucian
gentleman and drowned her confusion in another gulp
of her peach daiquiri.

She decided that if she kept her eyes focused away from Marcos, then the evening really was quite enjoyable. Despite Marcos's predictions, there wasn't any dancing—and for that she heaved a sigh of relief. That might have brought her in dangerous proximity to him. There was very little shop talk, and what there was was interesting.

As the first of the guests began drifting away, she had a smug feeling of having done quite well, thank you very much.

Roger was among the last to leave, and he drew her aside surreptitiously.

'Can I look you up back in London?' he whispered.

'Sure,' Beth agreed whole-heartedly.

'Just so long as I don't mind sticking to the rules of the game.'

She blushed and her face grew even redder when he placed a discreet kiss on her lips before leaving. A kiss that expressed affection rather than passion.

Even so, Marcos's voice behind her made her jump,

'Not a painful farewell, I hope?'

Beth turned towards him, too relaxed from her small share of daiquiris to work up the enthusiasm for an argument.

'Farewells are always painful when they're with someone you like,' she said lightly.

Wrong figure of speech. His eyes darkened. 'I wouldn't know,' he said silkily. Jane was lurking in the background, and he bade her goodnight in a voice that immediately hastened her departure.

She threw Beth a venomous glance and left.

'Perhaps,' Beth said, edging away, '**you don't like anyone.**'

'On the contrary. I like a lot of people.'

'But not enough?'

He lounged against the door-frame and surveyed her thoroughly through half-closed eyes.

'Depends on your definition of enough, doesn't it?'

'I think,' she said hastily, before she found herself treading deep waters once again, 'it's my bedtime.'

Marcos took her by her elbow, his touch sending shivers along her spine.

'I'll see you up.'

Oh, God, Beth thought desperately, this is playing with fire; please don't let me get burnt.

If only her damned body would listen to her.

CHAPTER SIX

THEY walked back to Beth's room in silence. She felt as though she were a piece of elastic, her nerves being stretched further and further with each step she took. At least they got her there in one piece, for which she was immeasurably grateful, although by the time she stood outside the door they were feeling distinctly wobbly.

She had already fished out her key from her bag, ready to make a quick getaway.

'Well,' she said, in a high, nervous voice which she tried to conceal with a little laugh, 'thanks for the lift—walk.' She fumbled with the key and felt him remove it from her fingers.

'Allow me,' he murmured, opening the door in one swift movement.

Beth stepped inside and then turned to face him, blocking his entry. If it was one place she did not want Marcos Adrino, it was within the confines of her bedroom.

She reached out for the key, mumbling a polite, Goodbye and wasn't it a pleasant evening? but instead of handing it to her he side-stepped her into the room and carelessly tossed them on to the small table by the bed.

Beth watched in dismay as he proceeded to prowl through the room, before finally stopping by the window and perching indolently against it, his arms folded across his chest.

This was not going to plan at all. She had not expected him to walk with her to her room, and she had even less expected him to barge in and install himself by the window.

She remained uncertainly by the door, not daring to take a step further, unsure what she should do now.

'You can close the door behind you,' he drawled, taking the decision out of her hands. There was a small smile on his lips, as though he could read exactly what she was thinking.

Indecision turned to anger and she slammed the door behind her, moving across to the sanctuary of one of the wicker chairs.

She had not bothered to draw the curtains before she had left earlier on, and outside the black sky was studded with stars. The silence between them was broken only by the background noise of the air-conditioning.

Beth looked at him, his dark eyes hypnotising her, blotting out her thought processes, making her mouth go suddenly dry.

'I'm awfully tired,' she ventured. 'It's been a long day. I really would like to get to bed now.'

'Feel free.'

'Without unwelcome spectators in the room!'

Her brief flirtation with anger was immediately quelled as he walked towards her, to be replaced by something that felt strangely like vertigo.

'This dress,' he murmured, standing in front of her, 'becomes you.' His finger slowly traced the outline of her exposed shoulders and her hair stood on end.

'Thank you,' Beth whispered hoarsely, edging away slightly.

'They say that you can tell a woman's personality by her wardrobe.'

'Do they?' She tried a nonchalant smile that immediately died on her lips.

'Mm. This dress, your bikini yesterday—they speak of quite an extrovert, daring personality. Are you?'

His hooded eyes bored into her. Something about his voice was like a low, seductive caress, and Beth fought it as hard as she could. She wasn't born yesterday. He was bored and, even though her morals left him cold, she attracted him.

Like a lot of men, she suspected that he had two standards. While it was all right for him to explore womankind, it was not nearly so acceptable for a woman to do likewise.

No, she was not his sort at all, but still he fancied her.

It was a purely physical thing. He specialised in that, didn't he? He used his sheer animal magnetism ruthlessly to get what he wanted, and who he wanted, and no doubt he saw her as easy game. After all, hadn't she, as far as he was concerned, slept with David Ryan and who knew how many others?

'It really is very late,' she said in a firmer voice, slipping away from him to stand pointedly by the door. 'Tomorrow we fly back, and I know I won't get a minute's sleep on the plane. I didn't on the way across. Maybe I'm allergic to travel. When I was young, I would always get car sick.' She was babbling. They both knew it.

He gave her a slow, predatory smile.

'You don't look terribly sleepy to me.'

'Don't I?' Of course I don't. With my cheeks all flushed, I know what I look. I look excited.

And she was. Her heart was beating quickly and she knew that if he laid another finger on her she would explode.

Had Laura felt like this with David? For the first time she could understand what had prompted her sister to sleep with him, disobeying company etiquette.

But wasn't that different? She was in love with him. Her mind suddenly shifted into overdrive and a wave of panic gripped her as she realised that what she felt for Marcos wasn't simply lust. It ran deeper than that. She was in love with him. She had flouted all her principles, all her well-meaning intentions, and fallen in love with him!

When did this happen? she thought desperately, staring at him with wide eyes. He had found cracks in her, insinuated himself, and now the realisation made her feel like a piece of driftwood being carried along by a torrent of water from which all escape was barred.

That was why, when he had touched her on the beach, her body had been set alight with desire. That was why she followed him with her eyes, and, when he wasn't around, with her mind.

'Please,' she whispered, 'please go.'

'Or else what?' he asked, moving towards her.

He rested his hand on the nape of her neck, caressing it in slow movements.

'Haven't you forgotten your company policy about relationships?' Beth asked weakly.

Her reminder had no effect on him at all. He didn't smack his forehead with his hand and smile apologetically, he didn't turn away from her brusquely. In fact he didn't do anything at all.

'I own the company,' he said huskily. 'I have my own set of rules.'

He raised his other hand to her head, tilting it upwards, then he kissed her eyes, his lips barely touching her skin, but nevertheless sending sweet electrical charges through her body.

'No,' Beth moaned, already regretting what had not yet taken place between them. 'You must go. Now.'

'Because you're attracted to me?'

She didn't answer.

'Don't try and kid me that you're not,' he murmured, taking her silence for denial. 'I know you are. I can feel it, but I want to hear you say it. Tell me that you want me.'

'You're very attractive, Marcos...'

'Tell me!'

'Yes!' she bit out. 'I want you. Now are you satisfied?'

'I will be.'

He brought his lips to hers, his mouth moving unhurriedly over hers, his tongue exploring the moistness of her mouth.

Beth shuddered, and then, in a gesture of defeat, brought her arms around him, curling her fingers in his hair.

Marcos gave a stifled moan and began to kiss her harder, until she heard herself whimpering against him, unable to stem the tide of passion welling inside.

She was hardly aware of him lifting her off her feet and carrying her towards the bed.

He lay her down, staring at her while he undressed, tugging off his shirt with impatient hands. Beth followed each movement hungrily.

'Now you,' he said, the bed sinking slightly as he lowered his body on to it. 'I want to undress you slowly. I want to touch every bit of you until I can't stand the agony of wanting any longer.'

He ran his hands along her thighs, gently pulling down her lacy briefs. Beth's legs parted. Her eyes were half closed now, her breath coming in quick little spurts.

She was moist and ready when his fingers began to explore the secret depths of her womanhood. The pleasure was intense.

Then he freed her of her dress, kissing the flat planes of her stomach, moving lower until she squirmed against him.

He was taking his time, inching her along bit by bit, so that the ecstasy was almost painful.

He trailed kisses along her stomach and then carefully unhooked her bra, exposing one full breast, the nipple hard with arousal.

His tongue flicked against it, and then, as though he couldn't himself stand the agony, sucked harder.

Beth felt as though she was burning up. She stroked his back roughly, arching as he kissed her neck.

'It's still a woman's prerogative to change her mind,' he murmured into her ear.

If only, Beth thought. In fact, if only this woman had had a shred of common sense in the first place.

'I would if I could,' she replied honestly, her eyes drowsy with passion.

'Good, because I don't think I would have been able to let you.'

He cupped her breast with his hand, massaging it, rolling the nipple between his fingers.

'Touch me too,' he ordered roughly, guiding her hand, and she felt a surge of power as she heard him moan.

She had never been touched by a man before, had never touched one, but her responses were not unsure. She was too feverish with desire, too caught up with the emotions coursing through her body, to feel anything but a desperate need for him.

She tensed slightly as he slid into her, and he stopped, frowning.

'I'm not hurting you, am I?'

'Of course not,' Beth replied. Not, anyway, in the way that you think.

He moved against her, fierce and assured, bringing her to a shuddering climax.

I had to lose my virginity one day, she thought sadly. What better way to lose it than to the man I'm in love with?

She tentatively stroked his stomach and he smiled.

'Don't. You might find that I have far more stamina than you think.'

'How modest of you.'

He chuckled and turned to face her.

'That's one thing I like about you,' he said, 'your sense of humour.'

'That and my body.'

'You're right, two things.'

Beth felt a surge of tears and blinked them away furiously. Hadn't she known that she would regret it? His lovemaking had demolished the last vestiges of her defences, leaving her vulnerable and exposed.

She had walked into it with her eyes wide open. Deep down, she must have known that he would have left if she had only said so. He was not the sort of man to force himself on a woman. He had no need. The world, she considered bitterly, could provide an endless supply for his taking.

He touched her cheek and she sighed.

'What was that for?' he asked curiously.

'What happened between us——' she hesitated '—what happened between us shouldn't have happened.'

'Didn't you enjoy it?' He kissed her ear, holding her hair in his fingers, and then blew gently into it.

'That's not the point,' she said, but already her arguments were weakening. He kissed the nape of her neck, his hand straying to her breast, and she relaxed against him.

'Then what is?' he asked huskily.

'There are things,' Beth said falteringly, 'things that you don't know about me.'

'And there are things that you don't know about me,' he pointed out. 'Why don't we just let nature take its course?' He caressed her thighs, parting her legs with his hands until she felt a feverish limpness invade her.

'It's not as simple as that,' she said. Half of her wanted badly to tell him the truth, but the other half informed her coldly that to reveal the truth would put paid to Laura's job and she would never again feel the sensuous delight that he aroused. He would turn his back on her in rage, she knew that, and now that he had opened this world to her, how on earth was she going to survive without it?

Sooner or later the truth would come out—that was as sure as the sun rose and set—but at least she could enjoy their temporary relationship and then, when the time came, she could make the inevitable departure.

Because inevitable it would be, whether or not this masquerade was happening. He was a man born to move on; why not take what she could, while she could? She would have a lifetime to recuperate, wouldn't she?

'I can't remember the last time a woman turned me on the way you do,' he murmured. 'I feel as though I can't have enough of you. Isn't that strange, all this time you've been working for me, and only now this is happening?'

'Strange,' Beth repeated faintly.

He was as aroused as she was, and this time their love-making was fiercer and harder.

Even in the air-conditioned room she could feel his body perspiring next to hers, and as he lay down beside her she traced her fingers along his stomach, feeling its dampness.

'Tell me,' he said, 'about Ryan. What do you feel for him now?'

He turned on his side to face her.

'I'd rather not talk about him,' Beth said quickly.

'Why not?' Marcos's eyes narrowed on her face. 'Does he still mean something to you?'

'Honestly,' she pleaded, 'can we drop the subject?'

'You're my woman now,' he said grimly. 'I want your thoughts to be on me and me alone.'

Fat chance, Beth thought despairingly, of their being anywhere else.

But the possessive arrogance in his voice stirred something in her, made her feel warm and heady.

'If we carry on this . . . this affair, could we still work together?'

'I could always fire you.'

'No! Don't do that!'

'You mean you value your job more than you do me?' he teased.

'Jobs are hard to come by these days.'

'And men aren't?'

'You're playing with words now.'

'So I am,' Marcos agreed silkily. 'I studied law at university. The habit of exploiting the English language has never quite deserted me.'

'That's terrible!' Beth joked, kissing him lightly, relishing her ability to arouse him. 'It means that you're never sincere.'

'I sincerely want to bed you over and over again,' he mocked, a lazy smile on his lips.

'You did mention your stamina...' She lay back on the bed, tempting him with her nudity, watching desire flare in his dark eyes.

'You wanton,' he moaned, bending his head to take her nipple into his mouth. Beth wriggled against him, urging his hands to explore other parts of her body that were also aching to be touched.

He was right, she was a wanton with him, totally lacking in inhibitions. She should be ashamed, but somehow when he touched her there was no room left for anything like that. He filled her horizons with his presence, he made a laughing-stock of all her moral guidelines. Most of all, he made her helpless.

If she weren't so damned helpless, then, she thought, she could tell him what needed to be told, she could find the strength to take the consequences.

Love more than hurt, it was agony—but it was irresistible.

As they boarded the plane the following day, Beth took one last lingering look at the timeless beauty around her and thought that St Lucia would always have a special place in her heart. It was there that she was found and lost.

They were discreet, but it was impossible to hide from Jane the fact that something had happened between them. There was a familiarity between them that hadn't been there before, and Jane's sharp eyes absorbed it all.

'You've slept with him, haven't you?' she accused acidly, when Marcos had left his seat for a few minutes.

Beth didn't answer. She didn't have to; the tell-tale flush on her cheeks said it all for her.

'Well, you got what you wanted,' Jane muttered, her eyes daggers. 'You bedded the boss. What were you hoping for? A pay rise?' She laughed shortly, 'Because he won't marry you, you know.'

The venom in her voice spurred Beth into self-defence.

'Nor would I expect him to!' she lied.

'Ha! Crack another one! All women hope for marriage, even someone like you. Not that you've had much luck. I mean, first David, now Marcos.'

Beth gritted her teeth together. Jane's words stung, because they were true. Admit it or not, she wanted Marcos Adrino for herself—not just for a week, or a month, or even a year, but for a lifetime.

'And what about you?' Beth asked quietly. 'Don't you want to get married?'

Jane flushed suddenly. 'Sure, but I don't intend to play the field until it happens.'

Beth didn't bother to object.

'Look,' she said earnestly, leaning across the aisle, 'maybe you're right. Marcos is inaccessible, and I'm a fool. But you don't have to be. You could find someone, someone to share things with. Isn't that better than clinging to a wild dream?'

It was a baldly honest statement, and Jane's face looked first surprised, then angry.

'You'll be sorry you ever got involved with him,' she promised. 'I'll...'

What she intended to do was lost on Beth, because at that moment Marcos reappeared, his eyes not taking in Jane at all, but hungrily dwelling on Beth until a surge of colour flooded her cheeks.

He slipped into the seat next to her and murmured, 'I don't think I've ever enjoyed a plane flight as much as this. Right now, I could take you. Maybe we could explore the more private regions of this plane together?'

'Not on your life!' Beth looked at him, horrified, and then burst into helpless giggling. The thought of finding somewhere on a plane private enough in which to make love was wildly amusing.

'What about if we spread a blanket discreetly over ourselves . . . ?'

'Somehow,' Beth informed him drily, 'I think we might be noticed. There are other people in this compartment, not least Jane.'

'Jane?'

'Your employee sitting across the aisle.'

'Oh, Jane. She won't notice a thing. Besides, she's glued to a magazine.'

A casual dismissal. Was this how he would speak about her once their affair was over? It was a fair chance that that would happen even before she had a chance to tell him who she really was, because she would tell him. Just as soon as she found the courage.

They chatted throughout the flight, but under the easy conversation his eyes were burning, devouring her. He touched her lightly, but just a fraction of a second longer than was necessary, so that she knew what was going through his head.

And she felt like a teenager, as though loving him had stripped her of her years and turned her into the vulnerable girl she had once been.

When they finally arrived back in London, it was an effort to drag herself away from him. Suddenly Laura's flat seemed like an exercise in isolation.

But Jane had resolutely hovered, determined to stay until she saw them leave on their separate ways.

Beth caught a taxi back to Swiss Cottage, dumping her suitcases on to the ground and heading for the telephone.

The time had come to put a stop to their little game.

Laura picked up the phone almost instantly, and Beth smiled.

'You weren't sitting on the phone, were you?' she asked lightly.

'Of course I was. Waiting for your call. How was it? Was it very hot?'

'Very,' Beth agreed. 'Hot and beautiful. Paradise, in fact. I could have stayed longer.'

'Well, I'm glad you didn't,' Laura said petulantly. 'I've been eaten with envy ever since you left. If you'd stayed any longer, you would have found my corpse in your flat.'

Beth laughed loudly. 'You eat too much to ever waste away from anything, including envy!'

'I could waste away from love,' Laura said seriously. 'I've tried, but I can't get David out of my mind. I just want to see him so badly... And especially now that I'm beginning to show.' There was a wistful sigh on the line.

'Laura, I've been thinking,' Beth said slowly. 'This won't work. I mean, my being here, pretending to be you. It was silly. No, more than that, it was reckless. We have to come clean, and then maybe you should get in touch with David, tell him about the baby; he has a right to know.'

'Never!'

'But...'

'Please, Beth, for me. Whatever you think of all this, you're in it now, and neither of us can back down.'

'Things have changed, Laura.'

'What?'

I'm in love with your boss, she had meant to say, but now she found that she couldn't admit it, not even to her sister. It was something she wanted to keep to herself for a while.

'I don't feel comfortable with this deception.'

'Please, for me.' She started to cry and Beth clicked her tongue impatiently.

'Don't,' she said sharply. 'All right, I'll keep silent for the time being, but I can't promise that I'll be able to stick it out.'

'Fair enough,' Laura conceded quickly, and Beth could see what was running through her sister's mind as clearly as if it had been written up in bold letters on a notice board. Laura hoped that she could persuade her to keep going, knowing, as Beth did, that the longer the charade continued, the more difficult it would be to confess.

Half an hour later, Beth hung up with the uneasy feeling that nothing had been resolved.

And something would have to be done. Things couldn't continue the way they were. Now that Marcos wasn't around, she could think more clearly, and she knew that she would have to gamble her temporary happiness on his understanding.

She unpacked lethargically and had a bath, afterwards standing for ages by the window and staring out, comparing the grey mournful skies outside with the brilliantly blue ones in St Lucia.

Had the sunshine gone to their heads? she wondered. Maybe it had addled them both, released some hidden spring, which would now slot back into place back in grim old England.

She tried to imagine life without Marcos and couldn't. It was just physically impossible to get him out of her head.

But the following day was work, and maybe the change of climate had already cleared her out of his system.

The thought continued to haunt her, right through the night, and on the journey in the following morning.

She told herself to be prepared, but by the time she let herself into the office her skin was already tingling with apprehension.

He was already in; his coat was slung over the coat-stand.

Beth slowly hung hers next to it, and blindly glanced down at the masses of post that had arrived in their absence.

Letters from abroad, inter-company memos, copies of engineering reports on some of their planned sites. She sat down and began sorting them out, half her mind on Marcos, just yards away from her behind his closed door.

When he finally buzzed her to bring him in a cup of coffee and to come with her shorthand pad, she heard herself replying in a crisp, distant voice. Not the voice of a lover. She had no intention of acting like a lovesick teenager, especially when there was a good chance that he had now relegated her to the category of the 'Brief Fling'.

He glanced up when she entered, then leaned back in his chair and surveyed her more thoroughly.

Beth absolutely refused to act coy. It was not her style anyway. She had always been a direct person; now she stared directly into his eyes and then sat down, her hand poised to take the dictation.

'Had a good night?' he asked softly.

'Fine,' Beth mumbled. 'I was pretty tired, though. How was yours?'

'Awful.'

She looked hesitantly at him, a flicker of delight coursing through her. 'Yes?'

'And you needn't look so smug.'

Beth controlled her expression, but she felt light-headed with joy.

'I didn't think I was.'

'I spent the entire night thinking about you, wanting you. In fact I was very nearly tempted to pay you a surprise visit.'

'Were you?'

'Is that all you can say?' But he shot her a sudden, charming smile that made her blood turn to water.

'No, there's an awful lot more I can say,' she informed him sincerely.

'Good, then you can say it tonight. I'll pick you up at eight.'

He returned to his work, quickly flicking through some folders on his desk, rattling off orders for her with his usual staccato rapidity, until she was happily lost in a whirlwind of work.

That was one thing about working for him; there was no time to daydream. He did not spare himself, and he did not expect his employees to do so, either.

Nor did he make any further allusions that day to the fact that their relationship was no longer the boss-secretary relationship. She didn't think that he really cared whether anyone knew about them or not, but on the other hand he had no intention of broadcasting it. And neither had she.

She was not given to sharing confidences by nature, and anyway her conscience wouldn't have allowed it.

As she dressed for dinner that evening, she felt the worry nagging away at the back of her mind. This charade had started out as a temporary game, a gamble to help her thoughtless sister out of a difficult situation and herself out of an unenviable rut after her own unsuccessful fling with Craig. Now it was much more. It had become a dangerous masquerade, with much more to lose than a job with a good salary.

Wilful Cupid had catapulted her into a dreadful nowin situation. To confess would be to lose Marcos, but to keep silent was only a cowardly way of buying time.

Her eyes flicked nervously as the doorbell rang, and she opened the door to see Marcos standing there, casually dressed, his black hair severely combed away from his face, a Harrods bag in his hand.

'I thought we were going to eat out,' Beth said, surprised, warming as he smiled at her slowly.

'Everything I want to eat is right here,' he drawled, shutting the door behind him. 'Cheese, salmon, salad and champagne. Courtesy of that fine department store.'

Beth grinned. 'How thoughtful of you.'

'And of course,' he murmured, coiling his long fingers into her hair and upturning her face to his, 'there's you. The most edible thing on the menu.'

His lips explored hers with leisurely sensuality, nibbling and teasing until she was gasping for breath. He pulled away eventually and said huskily, 'I've been waiting to do that all day.'

'That has a clichéd ring about it,' Beth said, but she was laughing, the nagging doubts conveniently put into temporary storage. She took the bag from him and they went into the cramped kitchen, his arms around her, his teeth gently nipping her neck while she chopped the lettuce and tomatoes.

'I'll never get this done!' she protested. 'Are you normally such a pest in the kitchen?'

'I'm hardly ever in one,' he said, picking up one of the kitchen implements and twirling it around as though it were some strange apparatus which he had never laid eyes on before.

'Haven't any of your girlfriends had them?' Beth asked curiously, averting her eyes because the desire to find out was stronger than she would have imagined.

Marcos shrugged. 'I expect so. I rarely ventured inside.'

'You surely didn't wine and dine them all of the time!' She thought of the elegant Angela Fordyce. No, she couldn't picture her in a kitchen at all. Maybe they liked a constant round of restaurants. As far as she was concerned, though, that thought held little appeal.

'Isn't that the standard courtship game?' he said flatly. 'I had no interest in the architecture of their houses apart from the obvious, and I certainly didn't want any of them cluttering up my apartment.' He had opened the bottle of chilled champagne and handed her a glass.

Beth regarded him soberly over the rim. Unintentionally, he was telling her what she already knew. That he was not a man for commitment. He liked change, and when the time came for her to confess all he would toss her out like useless rubbish. Except with me, she thought uneasily, it'll be far worse because his pride will have been affronted. God, why am I in this mess? But even as she asked the question the answer provided itself. She was in love with him, and doesn't love make cowards of us all? she thought. Wasn't it an addiction that made a fool out of good sense?

'Why not?' she asked, walking into the lounge. 'Don't you believe in love and marriage?'

'Do you?' The dark eyes scrutinised her face. 'Was that what you wanted out of Ryan?' His voice was hard.

'Marriage isn't on my agenda,' she said, avoiding the question.

'Then we see eye-to-eye.' He came and sat next to her, lightly tracing the contour of her body through her dress. 'Because I don't believe in marriage at all. All that stuff about love is so much hot air. I've seen enough failed marriages around me to last a lifetime. No, the only certainty is with yourself.'

'You mean your career,' Beth amended. He was at least being honest, but honesty hurt.

'I guess I do,' he said lazily. 'Women come and go, but without a career——' He shrugged. 'I've seen first-hand what happens, and that's not the way I intend to go.'

'And how long do you give us?' she asked, noticing that her hand trembled as she took a sip of the champagne. 'A week? A month? Three months maybe?'

'Who knows? Does it matter to you?'

'Oh, no,' she said bitterly, 'but if I knew, maybe I could plan my diary accordingly.'

He laughed at that, but she wasn't laughing at all. She wished she had never given him the opportunity for truth. Truth had a curious way of backfiring.

'You make me laugh,' he said, his eyes feverish as they swept possessively over her body, 'and that's a first for any woman. I'm prepared to live dangerously. Are you?' His hand cupped her breast, and under the thin cotton of her dress she felt her body hot with arousal.

Oh, yes, she thought, I'm living dangerously all right. More dangerously than you could ever imagine. Right now I feel as though I'm walking on a knife-edge, with two very sheer drops on either side. But until then . . .

She lay back on the sofa, breathing quickly as he unbuttoned the front of her dress, exposing her nudity to his hungry gaze, closing her eyes as his mouth found the hardened tips of her breasts.

Until then, I'll fill myself with you, my love, because it'll have to last a lifetime.

CHAPTER SEVEN

GRADUALLY Beth's life slotted into a pattern of love-making by night, while during the day no one would guess that there was anything between her and Marcos at all.

And every day she fell a little deeper in love with him. But that didn't stop the worry nagging away at the back of her mind. Every morning she woke up and thought, Today's the day, today I'll confess everything; but the thought of the immense void that his absence in her life would bring always made her good intentions die on her lips. So she kept silent, hating her cowardice, torn between the ecstasy of being with him and the agony of knowing that every minute brought her closer to the end.

And at work Jane continued to be a malicious threat hovering in the background, yapping at her heels like a little terrier that wanted to bite but found it maddeningly impossible.

She was in the office now, an irritating presence which Beth attempted to ignore by concentrating on her word-processor. Eventually Jane gave up her round of antagonistic questions and sullenly flopped into the chair facing Beth.

'I'm about to go to lunch,' Beth said pointedly.

'I didn't realise you ever went to lunch,' Jane said with staged incredulity. 'I thought you just stayed up here working and building up brownie points with Marcos.'

'I'll make sure that he gets those files you brought,' Beth said politely, changing the subject with accustomed swiftness. Jane insisted on angling every conversation back to Marcos, and particularly this morning Beth was not in the mood for it. She had too much on her mind.

'Still sleeping with the boss?' Jane enquired idly, juggling the plastic container with the pens so that they rattled irritatingly.

It was the very first time she had brought this out in the open, and Beth stared at her aghast.

'I beg your pardon?'

'You heard.'

'I thought I must have been mistaken.' There was a tremor in her voice which Jane seized upon with malicious glee.

'Would you like me to repeat the question?'

Beth snatched the irritating pen container out of Jane's hand and dumped it unceremoniously on the far side of the desk. 'There's no need,' she said tightly, 'because my answer's going to be the same anyway. It's none of your business. It never has been and it isn't now. So if you don't mind...' She began slipping on her cardigan, a rose-coloured one that matched her skirt and picked up the floral colours in her short-sleeved jumper.

'Marcos has changed, you know,' Jane said, an element of bitterness in her voice. 'He's not as caustic as he used to be, and he never, ever flirts any more. It's all your fault.'

Beth's mouth dropped open. 'I hadn't noticed any change in him,' she said without thinking.

'Well, he has, and it's all your fault. I suppose it's what you've been working towards, domesticating him.' Her tone was acidly accusatory.

'I really don't know what you're talking about.'

'You mean you don't want to know what I'm talking about. I——'

She was cut off in mid-sentence as the telephone began to ring, and Beth picked up the receiver with gratitude.

She didn't want to argue with Jane, she didn't want to be rude, but she knew that she would be if she remained a second more in the office.

Right now, her nerves were near to breaking and an unprovoked argument would just be the final straw.

'Good afternoon, Adrino corporation, how may I help you?'

She had hoped that Jane would vanish but she remained where she was, tapping her fingers lightly on the desk and staring around her. Waiting to resume her attack, Beth thought wearily.

There was a pause down the other end, then a man's voice whispered huskily, 'Darling.'

'Hello?' Beth asked, bewildered.

'My darling, don't you recognise me?'

'I think you must have the wrong number,' Beth said courteously.

Jane was staring at her now, intrigued no doubt by the one-sided conversation she was hearing.

'Laura, darling, it's me.'

At this Beth felt her body freeze. This was no wrong number. Whoever the caller was, he knew her sister, and the realisation of who it was struck her just as the man identified himself.

'Laura, it's me, David.'

'Oh.' Her voice had sunk to a whisper, and the colour had drained from her face.

She needed to sit down. She looked across and saw Jane looking at her with undisguised interest now.

Quite purposefully, she turned her back towards the girl, knowing that her action would probably only increase her curiosity, but determined that this conversation should not be overheard.

'You,' she said into the mouthpiece, 'what do you want?'

'Laura, darling...'

'Don't call me that,' Beth said sharply.

'Why?' David demanded. 'You still are. Despite everything. Look, we need to talk.'

'No!' There was definite panic in her voice now.

'Yes!' he spoke urgently. 'We need to talk! I'm in England...'

'Oh, God.' Hysteria was grabbing her by the throat. She didn't need this further complication in her life, not now. It was complicated enough already.

'I want to see you, Laura. I need to. Tonight. I'll come around to your place...'

'No!' She rested her forehead on the palm of her hand to stop it from trembling.

'Please, Laura. I have a lot of explaining to do.' Some of the urgency had left his voice now. He was pleading. She didn't want him to plead with her. She wanted him to go away.

But, she thought despairingly, it was not her place to send him away without a hearing. Laura would have to do that. Much as she hated it, she would have to agree to see him, and somehow get her sister down to London as quickly as she could.

Out of the corner of her eye she could see Jane avidly listening to as much as she possibly could, and she groaned inwardly.

There was a time when her life had been so simple, so uncomplicated. Now she felt as though she was walking a minefield.

'All right,' she agreed finally, 'tonight. At eight o'clock.'

Without giving him a chance to prolong the conversation, she hung up and swivelled around in the chair to see Jane smiling nastily at her.

'Who was that?' she asked casually, standing up.

'A girlfriend,' Beth lied coolly. 'Now, if you don't mind, I really would like to go to lunch. I'll see that Marcos looks at the files as soon as he's in.'

'Sure.' Jane smiled again, looking very much like a cat that had found some unexpected cream.

Beth didn't care any more. She just wanted to find some very dark, very private place, preferably on another planet, and leave all these problems behind her.

She spent the remainder of the day attempting to plough through her work, but her concentration was weak. Several times she found herself staring vacantly at the computer, her mind absorbed in her own problems.

Laura, as luck would have it, was uncontactable.

'She's gone to the doctor,' one of her colleagues informed Beth in a voice that implied that she was the unfortunate one who had got lumbered with the extra workload.

Beth knew what that meant. Trips to the doctor, as Laura had grumpily told her a few weeks ago, invariably meant a wait of anything between half an hour and two hours.

And then, after that, there was no guarantee that her sister would immediately return to the flat.

In fact, when she phoned at five-thirty, there was still no answer.

Weren't twins supposed to have some kind of un-canny telepathy? she wondered. If so, the invisible com-munication lines had definitely broken down in their case.

At least Marcos had not been in. He had flown to Paris for a breakfast meeting, and without him around she had had the freedom to give full rein to her dreadful foreboding.

She'd been a fool, she decided, as she travelled back to the flat that evening, for once oblivious to the chaotic crush of bodies against hers. She should have arranged to see him some other day, any other day. Jane, she thought miserably, hovering in the background, had not been conducive to rational thought at the time.

Anyway, there was no point debating the issue now. She had no idea where David was staying, so she couldn't cancel at the last minute.

She had just enough time, when she got back to the flat, to half-heartedly eat a bowl of pasta and have a quick bath when there was a sharp ring on the doorbell.

She jumped up from where she was sitting with a last, desperate wish that all this was some awful nightmare, and slowly opened the door.

During all the conversations she had had with Laura, her sister had only sketchily described what David looked like.

The man standing in front of her more or less fitted the description. Medium height, brown hair, blue eyes, and a face that looked as though it was on the point of smiling.

A nice face. Nothing like what she **had expected**. Men with nice faces, she thought, shouldn't behave like bas-tards. At least with Marcos you knew where you stood.

One look at that cold, arrogant, sexy face left you in no doubt that he could be a bastard if crossed.

Not so David. He was smiling now, extending a large bunch of flowers at her.

'Thank you,' Beth muttered uncomfortably, letting him into the flat with a sinking feeling of finality.

He brushed past her and then turned around, his blue eyes crinkling at the corners.

'You've had your hair cut,' he said, and she got the impression that he was as temporarily lost for words as she was, though for completely different reasons.

'I have a different hairstyle, yes,' Beth answered carefully.

She hoped that he would not do anything stupid, like try to kiss her, but, just in case, she walked away in search of a vase, dumping the flowers unceremoniously into it.

When she returned, she saw that he had taken off his jacket, which was damp, and had slung it over one of the chairs.

'You're wet,' she said bluntly.

'It's been raining. Hadn't you noticed?'

'No. It was fine when I left work earlier on.'

There was an awkward silence and Beth looked away.

'You don't seem terribly pleased to see me,' he said quietly, stepping towards her.

Beth efficiently stepped backwards. 'David, there's something that I need to tell you,' she blurted out in a rush, waiting for him to interrupt, but he didn't. He waited patiently and she thought again what a nice face he had. The sort of face that had, she reminded herself, seduced her sister into thinking that it matched the rest of him.

She took a deep breath, and began the tortuous explanation which she had always thought would have been directed at Marcos. The bizarreness of the whole situation rang in her ears as she heard herself trying to rationalise it, and when she had finished she didn't feel in the slightest cleansed by the confession. But then, she thought, she wasn't confessing to a man who held her life in his hands.

'But why?' was his only response, bewilderment creasing his forehead.

'That,' Beth said, 'has to come from Laura.' She stood up and began restlessly pacing the room. 'I'll phone and see whether she's in as yet, and get her to come down here as soon as she can.'

There was, she was pleased and relieved to see, no outburst of fury. His astonishment had swiftly been followed by calm acceptance. He obviously knew that there was a hell of a lot of explaining to be done, but he was prepared to wait for it.

She had no idea how she got through the next three hours. Laura, thank heaven, had been in at last, and had agreed to come down at once, her voice full of mingled anticipation and apprehension. Beth fixed David a light supper and stiltedly conversed with him from the opposite side of the room, unwilling to like him after what he had put Laura through, but finding it difficult to resist his easygoing good nature.

All the time she kept one eye on the clock. When the doorbell finally went, she rushed to her feet, pulling open the door, a smile of relief on her face. The smile froze on her lips.

Marcos was standing outside, still in his suit, although he had discarded the tie and undone the top button, and he wasn't smiling.

'Hello,' Beth said uncertainly, not moving from her position by the door.

'Surprised to see me?' he asked tightly, and without waiting for an answer pushed her aside and strode into the room.

Beth rushed behind him in dismay, standing still when she saw him stop in the middle of the room to stare at David.

'Ryan,' he said grimly.

David stood up, his only sign of embarrassment the reddish flush on his face.

'Marcos,' he said, 'I didn't expect you...'

'No, I'm sure you didn't. I'm sure neither of you did.'

He spun around to face Beth, his eyes narrowed with anger.

'I can explain...' Beth whispered miserably. But she couldn't. Not yet.

'Really,' he said icily. 'I'm sure you can think up something very interesting, but I'm not in the mood for fairy-tales right now.'

David's expression of bewilderment was growing by the minute.

'Marcos...' Beth began unsteadily, as he turned to leave.

Before she could complete the sentence, she felt his iron grip on her arm and she raised her eyes to his, inwardly cringing at the frozen black depths.

'You bitch,' he bit out softly. 'You bloody little bitch.'

'You're hurting me!' She tried to wriggle free of his grip, but he tightened his hand on her arm and she winced in pain.

'I could hurt you a whole lot more than this, the way I feel at the moment,' he said through gritted teeth, 'but you don't even deserve my anger.' With that he released her, and she staggered backwards.

The front door slammed behind him and she shot David a panic-stricken look.

'I'll be back in a while,' she whispered, grabbing her jacket and racing out of the flat before he could say a word. 'Laura will be here soon,' she threw over her shoulder.

Marcos was walking quickly towards his car, and even from a distance Beth could feel the rage emanating from him like something tangible.

She couldn't allow him to leave like this, not without any word of explanation.

She ran behind him, and he swung around to face her, the darkness of the night lending a frightening fury to his features.

She had never seen him like this before. She had seen his cold anger on that first day, and she had seen contempt, but she had never witnessed this chilling anger.

'Marcos,' she pleaded, her hand instinctively reaching out to him.

He thrust it aside, and stared down at her.

'How could you?' he asked, his face tight.

'It's not what you think,' Beth said, her face red with the misery of being in an impossible situation.

'No?' he jeered. 'You and he were just having a friendly chat, were you? Two ex-lovers discussing the weather and catching up on old news? Is that the line you're going to feed me?'

'Yes, as a matter of fact, we were just chatting, as it happens!'

'How cosy.'

'I had no idea that he was in England until today!' Beth said in a high, desperate voice. 'You have to believe me! He telephoned out of the blue and invited himself over!'

'And of course the word "no" doesn't exist in your vocabulary?'

Tears were blurring her eyes, making it impossible for her to speak.

'Lost for words, are you, darling?'

'Why won't you believe me? We haven't slept together. This is all a huge mistake. Who told you that he was here, anyway?'

'No, the only mistakes are the ones I've been blind enough to make.' Now he sounded as furious with himself as he was with her. She knew what he must be thinking. That he had been made to look a fool. 'And, if you must know, Jane told me what was going on.'

'Jane, of course.'

'I didn't want to believe her, but I had to find out, and it's just as well I came over, isn't it? Found out for myself just what type of woman you were. Tell me, would you have...continued to entertain us both? Or would you just have satisfied Ryan while he was over here? For old times' sake?'

She slapped his face at that, hard, the ringing sound creating a dreadful silence.

For a second, she thought that he was going to slap her back, but he didn't. Hadn't he said that she wasn't worth his anger?

His black eyes glittered.

'You're way off target!' she whispered urgently. 'You don't understand.'

'So where's the explanation, sweetheart? Make me understand. Isn't that why you rushed out here? To present me with some imaginative little story? Well, I'm listening: where is it?'

Beth looked at him in silence. Behind her she heard a taxi pull up outside the flat, and knew instinctively that it was Laura.

'You'll have to see for yourself,' she said. 'Please, Marcos. Please come with me.' Her voice broke, and, much as she hated it, she felt the tears streaming down her face, and she wiped them away with the back of her closed fist.

He remained as rigid as a rock, and she held her breath, waiting for him to tell her to go to hell, but he finally said coolly, 'Why not? Perhaps an amusing little story from you is just what I need. But it had better be amusing, sweetheart, or you'll find out just what it means to cross me.'

They walked back to the flat in silence and heard excited voices coming from within even before they had entered.

Beth slowly opened the door, watching as Laura and David disengaged from each other's arms, feeling Marcos's breath warm on her neck behind her.

'Here's your explanation,' she said with a sweeping gesture. Her eyes were still red from crying and she could hear her voice, laced with misery.

Laura's eyes widened as Marcos entered, but Beth hardly noticed. She was concentrating too intensely on Marcos's reaction to notice much else.

The shock registered on his face for what must only have been a matter of seconds, then it was replaced by cold inscrutability.

'Meet my twin,' Beth whispered. 'Laura. Your ex-secretary. I'm Beth, her sister.'

He caught on quickly, very quickly, but Beth was hardly surprised. His mental agility had amazed her in the past but she had slowly grown accustomed to it. He had a mind like a knife, able to cut through the unimportant to the heart of the problem.

Now his brain clicked into gear, and threw up the correct conclusion with astonishing speed.

He slowly turned to her, seeing her as though for the first time.

'A game,' he said with freezing stiffness, 'you two have been playing a little game at my expense. One pregnant sister decides to have her twin stand in so that she doesn't lose her job, is that right? Am I heading in more or less the right direction?'

Beth nodded mutely.

'I didn't want to——' she began, but he cut her short.

'Spare me your excuses,' he said coldly. 'Only a coward attempts to hide behind them.'

'She means it, Marcos,' Laura burst out. 'She never wanted to do this at all. I persuaded her, I used everything, even emotional blackmail. If you want someone to blame, blame me!'

One look from Marcos silenced her, then he returned his attention to Beth.

'Enjoyed it, did you?' he asked softly, with a twisted smile. 'Enjoyed taking me for a ride? Did you see it as a perverse kind of challenge? How long you could carry on the charade?'

'You're so wrong,' she murmured. Her misery had given way to a numbness, as though she had temporarily stepped outside her body, and was observing events from a distance. Even in her state she recognised the reaction as a kind of self-defence mechanism.

'A liar,' he drawled, 'a cheap little liar.'

There was a hush. Laura and David had retired to some other part of the flat, obviously knowing that what was happening between Beth and Marcos was not for their ears.

'I know what you must be thinking, and you're right. I lied to you, but only about my identity.'

She lifted her chin defiantly and he gave a short, cynical laugh.

'Only. Lucky old me. Well, you had your fun, and now I think I can find better things to amuse me.'

He turned to go and Beth caught hold of his arm, releasing it when he looked down at her hand distastefully.

There was so much more to say, but she knew with despairing certainty that none of it would get said now. He had made his mind up and who could blame him? How could he know that she had fallen head over heels in love with him?

'You don't want to try and understand, do you?' she asked. 'It's so much easier for you to believe the worst!'

'The facts speak for themselves, darling.'

'All right. I made a mistake. I should have told you, but I never found the opportunity.'

'Oh, no. There were no opportunities during all those times we were in bed together, were there?'

'How could I?'

He shot her a contemptuous smile. 'You're right. It would hardly have been an aphrodisiac, would it?'

'Stop acting as though your life has been unblemished!' Beth shouted, her misery giving way to anger. 'Stop acting as though you have the final word on everything that's sunshine and light! Are you going to try and tell me that you've treated the opposite sex with scrupulous fairness? That you've never made mistakes?'

'At least women knew where they stood with me. I didn't resort to the comfort of lies.'

'I had to think about Laura!'

'You had to think about yourself, you mean. You were here for a short stint. Why blow it when sleeping with the boss was so convenient?'

'You're acting as though I have no morals.'

'Well, from where I'm standing, they're not exactly shouting at me.'

Their eyes clashed and she was the first to look away, unable to find anything that would make him understand.

'And you would know all about morals, I suppose,' Beth intoned bitterly. 'Are you going to tell me that you weren't quite prepared to hand me my walking papers the minute I outstayed my welcome in your life?'

'Don't try and twist things round to suit your argument.' The dark eyes raked mercilessly over her face. 'Your behaviour was despicable.'

She stared mutely at him. 'I'm still the same person,' she said defiantly. 'Only my name's different.'

'You don't really expect me to buy that, do you?' he asked icily. 'You led me up the garden path. You conveniently avoided telling me the truth because, oh, dear, the opportunity never seemed to arise, and you stand there expecting me to forgive and forget?'

'No,' she muttered into the developing silence, 'I don't suppose I do. I know you well enough to realise that you don't forgive mistakes, even mistakes of the innocent variety.'

'You're damn right,' he said, his eyes knifing into her. 'And I don't forget, either.'

'That's nothing to be proud of,' Beth informed him dully.

'From where you're standing, I don't really think you can afford to say much on that subject, do you?' he asked with a contemptuous sneer. 'No, if I were you, I'd take a long, hard look at myself and then ask whether I'm qualified to give advice to anyone on morality.'

She looked at him, flinching at the glittering hardness she saw in his eyes. This was so much worse than she had ever expected. Had there been a ray of hope lurking in her subconscious that he might forgive her her sin of omission? If so, she was in no doubt now that any such hope had been sadly misguided.

'Do you want me to return to work?' she asked inconsequentially, realising that there was nothing to gain by prolonging their conversation. Nothing she could say wou ' ever wipe the disdain from his face. No one liked being deceived, least of all someone like Marcos Adrino.

He smiled again, cruelly. 'Oh, yes. You'll continue until I can find a suitable replacement, and you should count yourself lucky that I don't take legal steps to make you pay for what you did. You'll work for me, all right, and actually it might even be salutary for me to be forced to view my stupidity on a daily basis. They say that you learn from your mistakes; well, what better way for me to learn than to have my mistake staring me in the face every day of the week?'

This time he did not slam the front door, and Beth didn't follow him. There was no point. There was nothing left to be said.

CHAPTER EIGHT

BETH had no idea how she got through what little remained of the night. She blindly washed up the few dirty plates in the kitchen and then busied herself with tidying up the lounge, only looking up when Laura bounced into the room, full of life, her face wreathed in smiles.

Things, it transpired, had been sorted out between the two of them. Life was rosy and full of promise and her sister, true to form, was regaling her with her new-found happiness, thoughtless of the fact that all Beth wanted to do was find a dark corner and cry her eyes out.

Laura had never been good at facing other people's distress and, Beth noted wryly, she certainly hadn't changed in that respect.

She was on top of the world. David, Beth learned, had been miserable in Paris, had pined for her. And, more to the point, had no wife.

'He told me he was married,' Laura announced gleefully, 'he left the country, because he was afraid that he was getting too involved with me and he had never envisaged his life with a wife before. It daunted him. He didn't want to hurt me and he said he needed time to think, to put things in perspective. He's told me that if Marcos says anything about us he's quite prepared to quit his job and find another, anywhere I want him to.'

'So all's well that ends well.'

'You don't mind, do you?'

'Of course not!' Beth exclaimed sincerely. 'Why should I mind? I'm happy for you.'

'And you're all right?'

'Fine.' She managed a smile. Out of habit, she found herself sparing Laura her own misery, knowing that it would burst her bubble of joy, and wouldn't serve any purpose anyway.

Come what may, she had to carry on. Much as she wanted to, she couldn't take refuge in her room and weep until there were no tears left because that would be the pattern of her life for the rest of her days. She had to face the world bravely, even though she was cracking up inside.

Marcos, she told herself philosophically as she later stared at her bedside clock and tried to court sleep, was not designed to be hemmed in by a committed relationship. He was too much of a predator. She had known that all along. Surely that knowledge must make her burden easier to bear? If it did, it certainly didn't feel like it at the moment, though.

Right now she felt utterly hopeless.

She only wished that she didn't have to face him for the next couple of weeks, but perhaps it would strengthen her.

To her relief, he wasn't around when she arrived at work the following morning. She busied herself at the computer, but her mind was on the door, waiting for it to open, and, when it finally did, she felt her stomach constrict into a tight knot.

Marcos looked at her with a flat, unreadable expression and nodded coolly.

It was as though she were a complete stranger, and one with whom he did not particularly wish to acquaint himself.

He vanished into his office, buzzing her towards lunchtime.

Beth faced him across his desk with trepidation, wanting to see something on his face, some indication that she was on his mind, even if only in a negative aspect. But there was nothing and she realised that there would be no post-mortems on their failed relationship, no questions asked about her deception, no interest in anything she did.

When he spoke, it was about work and his manner was crisp and businesslike. He had told her that she didn't deserve his anger, and now she could see that as far as he was concerned she didn't deserve his contempt either. It was as though she didn't exist as a person at all.

It hurt. Underneath her bland exterior, as she carried on with her work, she was hurting more than she dreamed possible.

By five-thirty she felt as though she had undergone several years in a torture chamber.

She hesitated as she slipped on her cardigan, and then took her courage into her hands and knocked on his door. She just couldn't leave in this atmosphere of silence. She would prefer him to get angry with her, to rant and rave, anything rather than this.

He was studying some files on his desk when she entered, and he barely glanced up at her.

'I'm just off,' Beth said nervously, one hand still on the door. She felt as though she would physically crumble if she released it.

'Fine,' Marcos said politely. He raised his eyes to hers but the expression on his face didn't change.

Beth looked at him, trying desperately to see the man behind the mask. Her eyes followed the line of his powerful arms, arms that had held her, the curve of his mouth that had covered her body with kisses, the black eyes that had burnt with feverish passion.

'Is there anything you want before I leave?' Her words sounded embarrassingly provocative, even though they were not meant to be, and she carried on hastily, 'I've prepared all the information on those two hotels in North America. It's on my desk...' Her voice trailed off.

'No, you can go now.' He looked back down at the files on his desk and she felt a spurt of anger. All right, so she had been wrong, but how could he act as though they had shared nothing? He had not even seen fit to listen to what she had to say.

'Marcos...' she began.

He looked up at her and this time his eyes were hard. 'I told you to leave. Do I have to remind you that you take orders from me? The door is behind you.'

They stared at each other in silence, and Beth was the first to look away.

'Yes,' she mumbled, 'I'll see you tomorrow.'

'Goodnight.'

Beth had never known that she could miss anyone as she missed Marcos, but she did. She realised very quickly the following day that he had no intention of treating her in any way other than that of the polite, distant boss. Emotionally, he had dismissed her from his life, and his attitude rammed home the point far more forcefully than if he had sat her down and told her so himself.

On top of that there was the trauma of now sharing the flat with two other people, and, much as she loved her sister, she found that she preferred the privacy of being on her own.

To be fair, they were very easygoing. And blissfully in love. David had enthusiastically entered into the spirit of impending fatherhood, and they were both happily planning what they should buy, and when.

It was only when she returned to the flat after another endlessly long day at work that he informed her that he had lost his job.

Beth was staggered. More staggered than he appeared to be.

She stormed into work the following day, itching for Marcos to come back from his all-day meeting in Norwich, and when he did she quietly asked if she could have a few words with him.

'I have a lot to do,' he said, frowning, glancing at his watch, but she resolutely held her ground.

'This won't take long.' She met his eyes with that bland, icy expression which she had developed over the past two days, and he nodded curtly, preceding her into his office.

'Well,' he said, moving to sit behind his desk, 'what is it?'

'It's about David.' There was not a flicker of emotion in the black eyes, and some of her courage faltered. 'He's told me that he's been sacked.'

Marcos stifled a yawn, as though to imply that this subject could hardly qualify as being worth his valuable time.

'I'm sorry the whole thing bores you,' Beth said stiffly, 'but I don't think it's particularly fair to sack someone simply because of what's happened between us.'

'I did not sack David,' he informed her coldly. 'We mutually agreed that it was best for him to leave——'

'You sacked him.'

'And,' he continued, ignoring her interruption, 'if you think that this has anything to do with you, then you flatter yourself.'

Beth turned bright red. She could feel her nails biting into the soft flesh of her upper arms.

'Are you telling me that I meant nothing to you?' she bit out, unable to prevent herself.

He leaned back, folding his arms across his chest, and surveyed her without interest.

'I have no desire to discuss what...happened between us.'

'I can't agree to that!' Beth threw at him. 'Not when it affects someone else! Because I don't believe that David's dismissal had nothing to do with us!'

'I don't give a damn what you believe,' Marcos said in a courteous, conversational tone of voice, as though they were discussing the weather or the state of the economy. 'And as for your original question——' he picked up his fountain pen and tapped it lightly on the desk '—you meant to me what every other woman has meant to me. A brief liaison. Except,' he added, his eyes flint-hard, 'I don't normally part company with my women with quite such a sour aftertaste in my mouth.'

There was a heavy silence.

'No,' she pointed out bitterly, 'you prefer your women to have the sour aftertaste.'

'Is that what you have?'

He stood up and walked across to the window, staring outside, his back to her.

'Yes,' she admitted quietly. 'I have the sour aftertaste of someone whose side of the story hasn't really been heard.'

Marcos gave a dry laugh. 'And I thought that I'd heard all there was to hear on that little matter. Enough, at any rate, to last a lifetime.' He turned to face her, staring at her as though she had suddenly metamorphosed into some curiously disgusting specimen.

'I love my sister! That was the reason I agreed to the whole damn thing in the first place. I had no idea that I would become involved with you.'

'Oh,' he said sarcastically, 'you expect me to buy that, do you? You did it out of love. Well, heaven preserve me from that particular emotion if that's the sort of thing it inspires.'

His words cut her to the quick, but she would not show him that. If he wanted to treat her like a stranger, then two could play at that game.

'Yes, silly, isn't it?' she said coldly. 'Love can make us do all sorts of things that are totally out of character.'

'I wouldn't know. I have no siblings. As for love for someone of the opposite sex—well, that's unexplored territory, and will stay that way as far as I am concerned. Now, is that all? Or have you something else to get off your chest? If you have——' he looked at his watch '—you'd better do so quickly, because I have an appointment.'

'Far be it from me to stand in the way of your appointments,' Beth retorted.

She swung around to leave and saw the outer door open to admit Angela.

Beth stared at her, quickly covering up her reaction with an expression of coolness. But she was far from feeling cool inside. Her heart had flipped over in her chest, and she felt as though she could hardly breathe.

So this was his appointment. Some appointment. Why didn't he just say bed companion?

I really mean nothing to him, she thought with agony. As far as he is concerned, it's out with the old and in with the new.

Angela was smiling at her, although her eyes were all for Marcos.

She was a vision in pale turquoise, her hair loose this time and flowing over her shoulders. She looked as though she had been poured into her dress, an impression which even the casual jacket thrown over could not quite conceal.

'Ready, darling?' she asked Marcos. He nodded, his eyes flitting past her to where Beth was at her desk, her eyes averted, fumbling with her handbag.

She turned to face them, and as she did so she watched in horror as Angela lifted her face to his, and his dark head swept downwards to kiss her lingeringly.

Then he put his hand around her waist and addressed Beth with mild surprise.

'Oh, are you still here?'

No, she wanted to yell, this is just a figment of your imagination. 'I'm just leaving,' she said blandly. 'Have a pleasant evening.'

'Oh, we will,' Marcos promised softly. 'A meal, the opera, and then, who knows?'

At his side, Angela giggled coyly, her full lips forming into an instinctive pout.

Beth had the insane desire to strangle her. Instead she yanked open the door and walked quickly to the lift, hurrying just in case she was forced to share it with them. That would have been the last straw. It had been bad enough watching them drool all over each other in the office, but to have to witness similar displays of affection in the lift would have been unbearable.

She didn't go straight back to the flat. Instead, she walked through Knightsbridge, where the shops were all still open, browsing in front of the elegant store fronts, while her mind chewed over the image of Marcos and Angela like a dog with a bone.

Had he contacted her as soon as he had walked out of her life? The tears prickled behind her eyes and she blinked them away. She refused to spend her life weeping over a man who had told her in no uncertain terms precisely what she meant to him. And, as if that wasn't enough, had shown her.

'A meal, the opera, and then, who knows?' The words rang in her head relentlessly. Who knows indeed? From what she had seen, she knew exactly what they would be getting up to later on in the evening, and it certainly wasn't witty repartee and intellectual discussion.

When she had exhausted herself walking around the shops, she went to Covent Garden, where she found a little place to have a cup of coffee.

It was teeming with tourists. All full of life and going somewhere. Unlike her. Where was she going? Her life lacked direction, like a boat without a rudder on stormy seas. She was drifting in a world of pain.

It was after eight by the time she finally made it back to Swiss Cottage, and she breathed a sigh of relief when she found that Laura and David had taken themselves off for the evening.

She had no desire to speak to anyone at all, and rather than risk it she retired to bed early, and made a half-hearted attempt to read her book to sleep.

It was pointless. Her brain continued to worry the question of Marcos and Angela. She found herself looking at the clock, wondering what they were doing now, and it was only in the early hours of the morning that she finally drifted into a restless sleep.

She awakened the following morning, her body aching as though she was in for an attack of the flu, her eyes heavy.

The reflection that stared back at her in the mirror made her grimace. She looked as if she hadn't slept in a week.

She tried to hide it with some light make-up, and dressed carefully in her most sober lightweight suit.

She had gradually bought herself a wardrobe of clothes and was no longer dependent on Laura's, a fact which had made her smile, since her sister had no need of her own clothes now.

'You look dreadful,' Laura greeted her brightly when she finally emerged from her bedroom. David had already gone to an interview for a job in the city.

'You're so kind,' Beth replied.

'What's the matter with you?'

'What do you think?' Beth poured herself a cup of coffee, unable to face anything else.

'Marcos.'

'He's already found my replacement,' she said lightly. 'An older model but still in very good shape.'

'Why don't you leave?' Laura asked. 'You could return to Cambridge, you might even be able to go back to your old job.'

'And what about working my notice?' Beth asked. 'The last thing I need is to be given a bad reference.'

'He wouldn't do that! Don't be ridiculous. In fact——' she wrinkled her nose expressively '—I'm surprised that he's making you work there at all, given everything that's happened.'

'I'm not.' Beth drained her cup and reached out for her bag. 'I think he enjoys my discomfort.'

'Sadistic monster.'

Beth nodded and headed off. He's a sadistic monster, she told herself, so it should be easy to face him. After all, who goes weak at the knees when they're confronted by a sadistic monster?

He was already in when she arrived, and, for the first time in days, was whistling softly under his breath.

She sat down and he leant next to her, running through some of her day's workload, his arm very nearly brushing against hers.

Their proximity didn't seem to affect him at all, but it affected her. It was as if she was being subjected to some electrical charge which made her hairs stand on end.

'You seem in a happy mood,' she said icily, edging away from him, loading the paper tray with headed paper.

'Oh, yes.' He perched for a moment on the edge of the desk and Beth averted her eyes. 'Certain activities are so good for... relaxation.'

Beth's blood froze. It was an instantaneous reaction, but she recovered quickly.

'I'm sure.'

'And by the way, I'll be out to lunch. I probably won't be back until about three.'

'You have a meeting with some developers at three-thirty,' she reminded him, consulting the diary.

'I'll try and make it back by then. But if for some reason I'm detained, could you rearrange it for next week some time?'

'Of course,' Beth said stiffly. 'And will you be contactable while you're out of the office?'

He looked at her, his eyes glinting. 'Oh, I think the phone will definitely be off the hook for what I have in mind,' he said softly.

Beth looked at him with burning resentment. 'I already told you that it's not part of my job description to handle your personal life for you. I won't make excuses to your women and I won't make excuses to your clients because you've decided to be unavailable.'

'You'll do as I say,' he grated.

'Or else what?' she threw at him recklessly. 'You'll fire me? Go ahead!'

She had stood up, her cheeks flaming.

'Sit back down,' he bit out coldly, 'and I'll tell you this for free. While you're here, in my office, working for my company, you'll damn well do what I say, and you'll do it with a smile on your face. If you choose not to, well . . . references can be tricky things, can't they?'

'That's unfair,' Beth muttered, trembling.

'That's life.'

He leant across to retrieve a file from her desk, pausing over her with an icy smile. 'And have you finished the work on the St Lucian project?'

Beth shook her head.

'Why not? You've had long enough to do it.'

'I'll try and finish it by this evening.'

'Just so long as you do. Time is money, and I won't tolerate sloppiness in my secretaries.'

'Then why don't you hurry up and find another?' she muttered under her breath, and he cocked his ear as though trying to catch what she was saying.

'I missed that.'

'I said, have you had any luck with finding another secretary?'

'Oh, when I do, you'll be the first to know,' he informed her blandly. 'In the meanwhile, don't forget your instructions.' He threw her a calculatingly cool smile before going back into his office and firmly shutting the door behind him.

Beth wanted to scream. He was doing this on purpose, paying her back in the most effective way possible, and, much as she hated to admit it, it was working. She felt miserable.

He left the office at twelve-thirty promptly, sparing her only a brief nod, and she could quite happily have thrown her cup of coffee at him.

He was despicable, she thought. He was flaunting her replacement in her face and loving every minute of it. She had thought that nothing could hurt more than his cold silence, but now she knew that that was a bed of roses compared to what she was feeling now.

She ate a sandwich for lunch and pulled out a magazine, but the words blurred in front of her eyes, and she found herself thinking about Marcos and Angela with a ferocity that frightened her.

How could he be so cruel? His pride had been hurt by her deception, she knew that, but did he have to extract his pound of flesh in this way?

She could barely muster up the energy to be her usual friendly self on the telephone, and some of the customers with whom she had built up a pleasant chatting relationship over the past months could sense the change in her voice.

'Is there anything wrong?' one of them asked her with concern, and she felt like bursting into tears.

'No,' she said with effort, 'I must be coming down with something.'

'You need a holiday,' he joked.

I need amnesia, she thought miserably, agreeing with him light-heartedly and replacing the telephone.

When the office door opened at two-thirty, her stomach clenched and she waited for his entry. Would there be lipstick stains on his mouth? Maybe his tie would be dishevelled just that little bit, indicating what his lunchtime rendezvous had entailed.

She didn't think that she could bear another minute of this.

But it wasn't Marcos. It was Roger. A little thinner and a little browner, but with the same warm disposition that she had liked when she had first met him. And right now he was just what the doctor ordered.

I won't mention a thing about Marcos, she told herself, I won't say a word, only to find herself pouring her heart out to him five minutes later.

'Poor Roger,' she said shakily, mopping her eyes with the handkerchief he had given her, 'in the wrong place at the wrong time.'

'I don't know,' he said smiling. 'I'm told that I'm quite good at helping women who are carrying the world's problems on their shoulders.'

'Are you really? You own a scaffolding company, do you?' But he had done her a world of good, so when he pulled her to him she rested willingly against his warm frame, enjoying the comfort of his arms more than she would have thought possible.

It had been unbelievably comforting to pour her soul out to another person. True, she had briefly explained the situation to Laura, but her sister had been too wrapped up in her own world to spare her more than the barest cluckings of sympathy.

Roger, on the other hand, had listened. She felt the warm cotton of his shirt under her cheek and had an insane desire to remain where she was until the sharpness of the pain dulled a little.

She was only aware of another presence in the room when he whispered into her ear, 'Don't look now, but I think we've got company.'

She disengaged herself from his arms and saw Marcos staring at them from the door, his black brows meeting in a thunderous frown.

Before she could flee to the sanctuary of her desk, Roger had pulled her back to him, whispering under his breath, 'I think some jealousy might go a long way here.'

Beth cleared her throat meaningfully. Playing any sort of game with Marcos was not something she intended to do, but Roger was ignoring her and there was very little she could say.

'The joyous reunion,' Roger explained to Marcos with such bare-faced cheek that her lips twitched in a reluctant smile.

'I thought you were in the Seychelles,' Marcos said shortly, his eyes avoiding Beth's face. There was a dark flush to his cheeks.

'I was,' Roger said pleasantly enough, 'but something's cropped up and I had to see you personally.'

'In that case you can wait in my office.' His tone of voice implied an order and Roger obediently went through the connecting door, leaving Beth to face Marcos across her desk, oddly defensive.

'No wonder you have so little time to get your work done,' he said with icy hardness. 'You're obviously very easily distracted.'

At least my distractions don't take me out of the office, she wanted to retort.

'We must have been chatting for fifteen minutes before you came in,' she objected.

'I don't pay you to chat.'

Beth looked at the ruthless contours of his face without flinching. 'Shall I fax the information to the relevant offices once I'm finished with the report?' she asked sweetly.

'And you can wipe that smile off your face.'

'What smile?'

'I said that I don't pay you to chat.'

'Which is why I'm discussing the report with you,' she said calmly. 'After all, there's no point both of us wasting our valuable time here chatting, is there?' She stared at him with wide green eyes.

'You're treading a thin line, my girl.'

Beth gazed at him as if she hadn't the faintest idea what he was talking about.

'Were there any messages for me?' he asked curtly, as though her bland expression was beginning to infuriate him, and she smiled briskly.

'Two. I've left them on your desk.'

The look he gave her was sardonic. 'I'm surprised you managed to take any messages when you were so wrapped up in other things.' He looked pointedly at the connecting door to his office and Beth flashed another brisk smile.

Her colour had long returned to normal, and for the first time in days she felt as though she had slightly relieved herself of some of her nightmarish passivity.

'Oh, those calls came before Roger arrived.'

He leaned across to her and she automatically shrank back, not caring for the expression on his face.

'Keep your mind on your work, darling. Just don't forget who pays your salary.'

'How could I do that,' Beth asked with an innocent expression, 'when you won't let me?'

She could see that her control was getting under his skin. He didn't like that one little bit, she thought. He might have seen fit to toss her aside, to remind her with Angela's presence that she meant nothing to him, but that was his way of rubbing salt into an open wound.

He wanted her to respond. What he didn't want was her indifference. She smiled.

'I'd advise you not to keep Roger waiting,' she said blandly. 'You only have half an hour with him, then the rest of the day is booked with appointments.'

'Don't tell me what to do,' he snapped and she smiled again.

'Only doing my secretarial duties,' she murmured tonelessly. 'After all, we can't have any sloppiness, can we?'

He looked as though he could quite easily have hit her and she hurriedly focused her attention on the open file on her desk.

There was no point pushing this temporary triumph too far. But as he strode into his office, slamming the door behind him, she couldn't help thinking that at least the gods had meted out some victory to her, even if it was short-lived and changed nothing at all.

CHAPTER NINE

ROGER did not emerge for another hour and a half, and when he did Beth looked up at him and smiled. He winked back at her and strolled across to her desk.

'So,' he said with no attempt to lower his voice, 'about what we were discussing earlier on. How about it?'

Beth looked at him, bewildered, and he whispered conspiratorially, 'Do try and look as though you know what I'm talking about. I've got my back to Marcos, but I'll bet anything that he's listening to every word we're saying through that open door.'

Beth glanced past Roger, and to her surprise he was right. Not only was Marcos listening to them, he was also staring at them broodingly.

'Well?' he prompted.

'Well, what?'

'How about it?'

'Sure.' She flashed a wide smile, not having the faintest idea what she had agreed to. Lowering her voice, she hissed, 'I don't think this is a very clever idea, really, Roger.'

He ignored her whispered plea. 'So I'll pick you up at eight, then?'

Beth nodded in resignation, and Roger grinned encouragingly. 'Be sure and put on the glad rags, my beautiful; I think we'll paint the town red tonight.'

With that he left the office, a smug smile on his face. Well, he was certainly having fun with his little idea for

154

arousing Marcos's jealousy, but she didn't like it one little bit.

She had had enough schemes to last her a lifetime. Still, it would be nice to go out with Roger for a change, instead of moping around the flat, which seemed to be how she spent most of her leisure time these days.

Marcos's voice, crashing into her introspection, startled her.

'Now that your social gathering has disbanded,' he said in a voice heavy with sarcasm, 'would it be asking too much for you to come in here and apply yourself to a little work?'

Beth obediently trotted into his office and sat down, barely catching her breath before he began barking out his dictation to her, indicating sections on the various reports which she needed to identify, yet giving her hardly enough time to make the necessary notes.

After ten minutes her wrist felt as though it was on the verge of dropping off, and she interrupted him politely, 'Would you mind slowing down a bit?'

Marcos leaned back in his chair and inspected her with infuriating thoroughness.

'Going a bit fast for you, am I?' he asked in a dangerously innocent voice.

Beth recognised the tone instantly. She had heard it used often enough with certain members of staff whose attitude to their work did not happen to conform to his, and it usually preceded one of his bitingly critical attacks.

She eyed him warily, not knowing what sort of response the situation demanded.

'I've reached the bit about the targeted profits,' she began, deciding that she couldn't go too far wrong if she stuck like glue to the subject of work.

'Maybe,' he said in a falsely conciliatory voice as though she hadn't spoken, 'your mind is elsewhere.'

Beth schooled her features into a look of uncomprehending blankness.

'Dear me, have I lost you?'

'My mind wasn't elsewhere,' she objected truthfully, abandoning her stab at pretending that she didn't know what he was talking about.

'Well, you've never had a problem keeping up with me before.' He looked down at the sheafs of paper on his desk and absent-mindedly began leafing through them.

'Still,' he carried on in that voice that was forbidding yet patronising at the same time, 'no doubt you were wrapped up in your plans for this evening with Roger. How exciting for you to be renewing your old friendship.' He uttered the word 'friendship' as though it were one of the seven deadly sins.

He's jealous, she thought suddenly. She felt a brief moment of delight and then just as quickly stifled it. What was there to feel delighted about?

He might be jealous, but it wasn't because he cared two hoots about her. Oh, no. He was jealous because he might no longer want her, but he didn't care for the thought that she might be switching her attentions to someone else. That didn't fit in with his plan to torment her at all. He wanted to have her attention all for himself, so that he could parade Angela in front of her with shameless blatancy.

'Yes, it's very nice seeing Roger after all this time,' Beth responded offhandedly, noticing the grim hardening of his features. 'We got on like a house on fire in St Lucia.'

'Did you really? And now you plan on slotting him into your life on a more...rewarding basis?'

Beth opened her mouth to deny any such thing, and then closed it. Why should she protest her innocence? Why should she give him the satisfaction of suspecting that she had eyes for no one but himself. He probably knew that already anyway, but she damn well wasn't going to confirm it.

She shrugged eloquently and stared at her typing pad.

'I hate to disappoint you,' he ground out, 'but he won't be in the country for more than a week at the most.'

'An awful lot can happen in a week,' Beth pointed out mildly. 'Is there any more dictation or can I return to my desk now?' She smiled at him and he scowled.

'I might have guessed,' he said coolly, 'that you would start playing the field once you had gained a little experience.'

Beth turned white. 'And what exactly is that supposed to mean?'

He shrugged. 'Merely an observation. Women who have spent their lives in physical hibernation often show a tendency to break out once they've tasted what they've missed. And you weren't exactly practised when we first met, were you? Sure, you might have had the odd boy-friend, but none of them did anything for you, did they?' He held his fountain pen up and inspected it. 'In fact, no one did anything for you until I came along.'

There was a thick silence and she wished that the ground would open up and swallow her.

'That's the most arrogant thing I've ever heard in my life,' she muttered in a strangled voice.

'But true, admit it.'

He was staring at her intently, assessing her.

'I don't admit anything of the sort,' Beth threw at him bitterly, 'but maybe you're right about one thing. Maybe I have decided to break out, not that it would be any of your business if I did. As for your generalisations on the female race—well, you should know, shouldn't you? After all, you've slept with enough of them.' And still are, she thought. Or at least with one of them. Angela Fordyce.

'Does that bother you?'

'No!' she lied, snapping shut her typing pad. 'Why should it? And I thought you disapproved of my squandering my working time by chatting? I thought you made it clear that I was paid to come in here and work?' She stared pointedly at her closed typing pad. 'This conversation hardly falls into the category of work, does it?'

He ignored her outburst. 'Roger's not your type.'

'How would you know?' She was beginning to feel hysterical and trapped at this turn in the conversation. How dared he just sit there and act as though he had any kind of control over her life, when he had discarded her without a backward glance? Arrogant, she thought. Hadn't I always known that?

'You'd eat him alive,' Marcos was informing her casually. 'Does he know that underneath that cool little exterior there's a wildcat with a tongue like a razor?'

Beth stood up abruptly. 'I don't have to stay here and listen to any more of this,' she remarked tightly.

Marcos shrugged, his expression unreadable.

'Off you go to do your typing and plan your romantic little evening with him, then. Don't forget, though, that the office party is tomorrow evening, and I'll expect you to be there.'

Beth stared at him blankly. She had forgotten that office party completely. It had been one of those affairs arranged months ago, and with everything that had been going on it had slipped her mind totally.

'So,' he murmured, reading her expression, 'just don't go making any arrangements.'

'I won't,' she snapped, then added with a wicked sense of pleasure, 'Not that it makes much difference. Roger can come to the party with me, can't he?' She flashed him a bright smile. 'So if you'll excuse me I'll just go and start my typing and plan my little romantic evening with him, and, while I'm about it, I'll also plan my romantic little evening tomorrow night as well. After all, office parties can lead to all sorts of things, can't they?'

She turned and walked towards the door, her head held high, half expecting him to summon her back in that peremptory tone of his, but he didn't.

She closed the door quietly behind her and exhaled a long breath.

How much longer could she stand working for him? Just when she thought that things could not get more unbearable they did. I should walk out, she thought, and take the consequences. Except…except life without Marcos around, even a Marcos who could reduce her to tears, was no life at all. Wasn't that why she had been prepared to remain here and work out her notice?

She left work promptly at five-thirty. There had been no more accusations or innuendoes. In fact he had not made any more personal remarks to her for the remainder of the day, his eyes only flicking cursorily over her as she got ready to leave.

She staggered home after delays on the Underground, and spent at least an hour bathing and dressing very carefully. She was determined to have a good time with Roger if it killed her in the process. She was also determined not to think of Marcos at all. In fact, she had devised what she considered a pretty effective way of dealing with the problem. Every time that dark image began creeping into her thoughts, she would immediately focus all her attention on an imaginary scene on a beach somewhere until she felt that the image had safely receded into the background.

It didn't work, of course. Charming though Roger was throughout the evening, her mind insisted on throwing up graphic images of Marcos at the least expected moments, and there was nothing that she could do about it.

Roger, at any rate, had been thoughtful enough not to mention him at all until they had arrived back at her flat.

'Did it work?' he asked curiously and Beth grimaced.

'It was a stupid idea,' she said ruefully, not bothering to feign ignorance.

'Well, there's always tomorrow night.'

'Tomorrow night?'

'The office party.'

'Whoa!' Beth laughed and raised one restraining hand. 'No high jinks at the office party!'

'Would I?' Roger grinned impishly at her and looked offended.

But his little scheme gave her a nervous feeling in the pit of her stomach. He might not realise that playing games with Marcos was a dangerous pastime, but she did. Marcos had a unique set of rules for himself and could be quite ruthless if anyone infringed them.

She spent the next day counting the minutes until it was time to leave, guiltily realising that she was actually looking forward to the party because it meant that she would be provided with an extra opportunity to be in his presence.

With a lot of nagging from Laura, she finally gave in to her sister's choice of dress for the party. A jade-green affair that looked several sizes too small.

'Go to that party and stand out,' her sister had instructed her firmly. 'Make a show of pretending that you're on top of everything.'

Beth had eyed the outfit sceptically. 'In that dress, I'll look as though I want to be on top of *everyone*,' she had commented wryly.

But she had given in, and, she had to admit to herself, it didn't look half bad. It was shoulderless and hugged her body, finishing just above the knees. She stepped into a pair of high-heeled black shoes, brushed her hair until it gleamed in a straight curtain just below her chin, and batted her eyelashes coyly when Laura shrieked in glee at her creation.

Roger was as enthusiastic as well, and by the time they arrived at the London hotel which had been booked for the party Beth was feeling distinctly buoyant.

The place was already teeming with people. Most of the faces she either knew or else recognised, and she happily allowed herself to be absorbed in the throng, conscious of the stares she was receiving from some of her male colleagues.

It was always an eye-opener to see people out of their work clothes, and she knew that some of them were looking at her in a new light, asking themselves whether this was the same soberly dressed, efficient secretary on the top floor. Many of them were new and had only seen Beth, not Laura.

'You're the belle of the ball,' Roger whispered to her when they found themselves alone together by the bar. 'What I want to know is, where is the big man himself?

Shouldn't he be here by now? In fact, he should have been the first person here!'

'Since when has Marcos ever conformed to rules?' Beth asked lightly.

She had already found herself scanning the room for him, much to her irritation, relieved and disappointed at the same time when she did not see him anywhere.

She was about to order a drink at the bar when she heard Roger murmur at her shoulder, 'About time,' and she swung around automatically, spotting him instantly at the door to the salon.

He stood out in any crowd, but tonight he looked superb. He was in evening dress, and the impeccable black cut made him seem taller than usual, his shoulders broader. He was chatting to one of the other managing directors, his eyes cool and watchful even though his lips were curved in a smile at what was being said, and Beth felt her breath catch in her throat.

She watched him compulsively as he turned to the door, obviously waiting for someone else, and she saw Angela Fordyce enter, dressed in a black dress that screamed expense.

'The other woman?' Roger enquired at her shoulder and Beth nodded.

She told herself sternly that she was not in competition, but she felt a thread of jealousy surge through her veins and she had to look away.

'You're far more interesting-looking than she is,' he assured her comfortingly, and Beth laughed.

'That's a questionable compliment, but thank you anyway.'

She gulped down some of her drink, and made a big effort to listen to what Roger was saying to her. She made

an even bigger effort not to indulge in her stupid need
to scour the room for Marcos's dark, handsome face.

It was difficult but she succeeded. Her natural instinct
had always been to keep her emotions to herself, and
for once it stood her in good stead. By the end of the
evening she could have individually counted Roger's
eyelashes, but she didn't mind because she had succeeded in ignoring Marcos's presence completely.

Around her, the music, which had started some while
ago, was blaring out. Roger had taken her hand and was
leading her to the dance-floor. It was not where she
wanted to be. Marcos was there, with Angela, and she
wanted to be as far away from them as was physically
possible in the room. Annoyed with herself, she eyed
them covertly across the shadowy crowds of people. Her
eyes locked with Marcos's and she felt her heart skip a
beat.

When the music came to an end and she realised that
he was walking towards her, her mouth went dry and
she turned frantically towards Roger.

'Shall we get ourselves another drink?' she asked,
taking him by his elbow.

'You wait here,' he instructed. 'I'll get something for
you. What will you have? More of the same?'

'No,' Beth said hurriedly. 'Yes. I mean, I'll come with
you.'

Marcos was approaching her and she just wanted to
escape, even though she knew that she was reacting like
a silly schoolgirl. After all, she could hardly avoid him
for the rest of the evening, however much she would
have wanted to. It would look highly odd to say the least.

But she couldn't face him. Not yet. Maybe after
another drink.

'Don't be silly,' Roger was saying, immune to her pleading look. 'Pointless both of us battling our way through this crowd. No, you save our spot on the dance-floor and I'll only be a minute.'

She watched helplessly as he was eaten up by the people, spinning around when she heard Marcos's voice behind her.

'Care to dance?' he asked softly, as the music began. Another damned slow number, as luck would have it.

Up close he looked even more devastatingly sexy than he had from a distance.

Beth dragged a smile to her lips and shrugged.

'I've had more enthusiastic responses to an invitation to dance,' he drawled, enfolding her in his arms until she felt as though she was going to faint.

She had slept with this man, knew every inch of his body, and, right now, her own body was reacting just as it always had when it was close to his.

Under the stretchy knit of her dress, her breasts felt painfully sore, and she knew that as they rubbed against the stiff material of his dinner-jacket the nipples were hardening in response to his nearness.

'Perhaps you ought to find a more enthusiastic partner,' she replied tightly, and his body stiffened.

'No doubt you can't wait to get back to Roger,' Marcos responded in a hard voice, 'but what would people think if the entire evening passed and the boss didn't once dance with his secretary?'

'Since when have you ever cared what people thought?' Beth pointed out. 'And, since you claim to be so concerned by other people's opinions, what will Angela think?'

He laughed under his breath. 'You're right. I don't care what people think.'

He pressed her harder against him and a quiver of alarm shot through her.

She didn't want him to suspect what kind of response she was having to him. Let him think that she couldn't wait to return to Roger's arms. If he thought that, then it afforded her some protection, because she wouldn't put it past him to play a cruel little game of arousing her, only to smile mockingly and walk away.

'Well, I happen to care a great deal what Roger thinks,' she informed him in as controlled a voice as she could muster. She glanced around for Roger who, as luck would have it, was nowhere to be seen.

'Do you?' Marcos's voice was lazy, but with a edge of something which Beth couldn't quite recognise. 'Why? Have you slept with him?'

'What?' She pulled back and met his black eyes.

'I asked whether you're lovers.'

How nice if I could lie to that one, Beth thought resentfully, but that would have been taking the game one step too far.

'That doesn't deserve an answer,' Beth said tautly.

'You haven't,' Marcos said with a note of satisfaction in his voice, and she could have hit him. He was looking down at her and she stoutly refused to meet those dark, sexy eyes. 'Enjoying the party?' he asked lazily, one hand moving to the nape of her neck, the feel of his fingers making the fine hair stand on end.

'It's very nice,' Beth remarked, holding on to the control in her voice with effort. 'The food was very good, as was the company,' she added pointedly. 'Everyone seems to be having a good time.' That's it, she thought. Keep it polite and you won't run into any difficulties.

'Don't they?' he murmured into her hair. 'And who do you think is going to end up in bed with whom?'

His words brought a heated flush to her cheeks. 'I haven't the faintest idea,' she said evenly.

'Jane and that accountant chap, I think,' Marcos mused. Beth didn't answer, but she inwardly agreed with him. The two had been inseparable since they arrived and it had crossed her mind that at least Jane had had the sense to do what she herself had found so difficult. Namely, cure herself of her addiction to Marcos.

She shrugged. 'Is that the point of office parties?' she eventually asked.

'As you informed me, they can lead to anything,' he said softly, 'but not with you and Roger, I don't think. Even though you've spent the entire evening with him. Don't you know that one of the duties of a good secretary is to socialise at these types of things?'

'Please don't start lecturing to me on the fact that you're paying me to do my duty. I happen to enjoy Roger's company.'

'And I thought that you were avoiding me,' Marcos whispered, amusement in his voice.

What was this all leading to? Beth worried. Had he been drinking?

'You were wrong, then, weren't you?'

'Was I? I've been looking at the two of you. Body language is so interesting, don't you agree? I would have said that, out of this entire lot of people here, you and Roger are the least likely to end up in bed together, however much you try to convince me that it's a possibility. You haven't slept with him, and you won't. And we both know why, don't we?'

The music seemed suddenly very loud and Marcos's grip on her was stifling.

She tried to hang on to her self-control, reassured herself that she could handle whatever little innuendoes he threw at her, but she could feel her heart thudding in her chest and her skin had broken out in a fine perspiration.

'You don't expect an answer to that question, do you?' she asked tightly, when the silence between them threatened to overwhelm her. It infuriated her that he felt himself authorised to make sweeping statements about her sex life. No doubt he wanted her to admit that she was still deeply attracted to him, that no, Roger meant nothing to her. He wanted to hear everything he said confirmed, so that he could torture her with Angela at his leisure, secure in the knowledge that his method of extracting revenge for what she had done was working.

Body language, she thought acidly. Looking at the body language that had been going on between Marcos and Angela left her in no doubt that bed was their final destination.

'No,' he said lazily, 'I don't, as a matter of fact. You would only be confirming the obvious, because it's me you still want. It's written all over you.'

'How dare you?' Beth whispered impotently. The song was drawing to an end, and she pulled away from him, her eyes stinging with anger and humiliation.

Roger was weaving his way back to her, drinks in his hands, and she turned to him with the enormous relief of someone lost at sea who suddenly spied a ship on the horizon.

'Thank you for the dance,' she said through stiff lips, turning away before he could suspect what his amusing little observations had done to her.

She walked blindly towards Roger, her body shaking with emotion.

'What's the matter?' he asked, concerned. He held out the drink for her, but Beth shook her head violently.

She didn't want a drink; that wouldn't cure anything at all. What she wanted was to get away, far away. It dawned on her that there was no point in torturing herself any longer. She would flee back to Cambridge and try to rebuild the shattered pieces of her life. Tomorrow. She would no longer give him the satisfaction of playing his amusing little games at her expense.

'I don't feel terribly well,' she whispered, pulling him a little to one side. 'You stay. I can take a taxi back.'

'I wouldn't dream of it,' he said stoically. 'I'm your escort. Besides, who knows what I would get up to if you weren't chaperoning me?' She could see that he was puzzled at her behaviour, but he wasn't asking any questions, and for that she was grateful.

He took her hand and they threaded their way towards the exit with as little fuss as possible.

In her head she was already wondering what time the earliest train out of London was. Whatever time it was, she would be on it, even if it meant leaving half her clothes unpacked.

They were ready to leave when a soft voice said beside her, 'Going somewhere?'

'Marcos!' Roger grinned and Marcos ignored him, staring at Beth instead. She could almost hear his brain clicking away, working out the reason for her sudden departure.

'Home,' she replied coolly. 'I have a bit of a headache.'

'That was kind of sudden, wasn't it?' Marcos murmured. 'You seemed all right a moment ago when we were dancing.'

'These things do come on suddenly.' Was it her imagination, or was there a hint of smugness in his voice? All of a sudden, she just felt horribly tired.

'Come on, Roger.' She linked her fingers through his and turned to walk away, when Marcos's hand gripped her arm like a vice.

'Not so fast,' he said tautly.

'Let me go!' Beth snapped, furious now at his arrogance. Haven't you had enough of your cat-and-mouse game with me? she wanted to scream.

Roger was looking awkwardly at them both and Marcos turned to him with a snarl.

'Go back to the party, I'll take her back.'

'I do not want to go anywhere with you!' Beth all but shouted. 'Now take your hands off me!'

His fingers were digging into her flesh, making it impossible for her to move. As if suddenly realising that he was hurting her, he relaxed his hold slightly.

'I told you I'll take her back,' he repeated to Roger. 'And that's an order.'

'I'll be fine, Roger,' Beth said, defeated, knowing that he was unsure what to do and not wishing to prolong his embarrassment further.

'Sure?'

'What the hell do you think I'm going to do with her?' Marcos bit out. 'Now clear off!'

He more or less dragged her through the door, collecting her jacket from the cloakroom and tossing it over her shoulders.

'How dare you talk to Roger like that?' Beth asked angrily, as soon as she had recovered her power of speech.

'He works for me!' Marcos thundered, his brows knitted in a dark frown.

'That doesn't give you the right to push him around!' She yanked her arm away from him. 'And I do not want to go anywhere with you!' She began walking quickly towards the taxi rank.

His lean hand shot out, stopping her in her tracks and she raised furious eyes to him. 'Let me go! I'm not going anywhere with you, I told you! I'd rather throw myself under the nearest bus!'

'They don't run at this hour.'

'Hilarious!' she yelled, looking at him. 'What a sense of humour! You missed your calling as a stand-up comedian! Now, if you don't mind, go away.'

'I do mind.' His voice was harsh and it flashed through her mind that he was not nearly as controlled as he seemed to be. Right now, though, the last thing she felt inclined to do was analyse his state of mind. She didn't care what it was. She only cared about reaching the safety of her house, without him.

'Well, isn't that sad?' she bit out. 'But frankly I don't care one way or another.' She wrenched herself free of him and shouted, 'You're a bastard, Marcos Adrino!'

'You made me that way!'

There was a silence and then he reached out, pulling her towards his car, opening the passenger door and pushing her into the seat.

She was hardly inside the car, when he accelerated away from the pavement, tearing along the London streets until they finally pulled up outside Laura's flat.

The journey seemed to have been accomplished in five minutes. One minute they were screeching away from the hotel entrance, the next they were outside the flat, and during that time not one word had passed between them.

Beth had been too caught up in her thoughts, too angry at his arrogance, and he had been wrapped up in his own thoughts as well. She turned to him, her hand on the door-handle.

'Goodbye,' she said stiffly.

She pushed open the car door and she watched in horror as he stepped out of the car, his hands in his pockets, his foot idly kicking the car tyre.

'I can see my way to the front door,' she informed him icily. 'You've done what you set out to do. You've chauffeured me back to my flat; now just go away!'

Their eyes tangled and Beth felt a shiver of panic course through her.

She looked away and he gripped her chin with his fingers, forcing her to look at him. 'Dammit, woman,' he countered furiously, 'look at me! Can't you see what you're doing to me?'

CHAPTER TEN

BETH stared at the commanding dark face reluctantly.

'What do I do to you?' she asked shakily. 'As far as you're concerned, I'm a liar, beyond contempt, and you've made no effort to conceal the fact that as soon as I was out of the way you couldn't wait to...' Her voice felt as though it would break at any moment and she took a deep, steadying breath. 'To jump into bed with someone else.'

She turned away and fumbled with the key, finally managing to insert it into the lock, and with one quick movement she pushed the door open and tried to slip inside. But Marcos prevented her from slamming the door shut behind her, which was what she had in mind, by barging his way in.

Beth watched in growing dismay as he prowled restlessly around the room, finally standing still by the window and turning to face her.

'Where's your sister?'

Beth shrugged, not moving. 'In the bedroom, I expect. Sleeping.' Which, her tone implied, is what I want to be doing right now. Were it not for you.

She gazed miserably at him, drinking in the hard contours of his face, wishing that she could be more in control of her emotions so that she could handle this situation with aplomb.

'I really would appreciate it if you left,' she said finally, when the silence stretching between them was beginning to make her nerves fray even more at the edges than they already were.

Her feet were beginning to tingle with pins and needles from her rigid position by the door and she hesitatingly walked across to one of the chairs, sitting down and staring in alarmed fascination as he approached her. He moved unhurriedly, but even so she felt as though she were in a net, and there was nothing she could do to escape.

Not that she could run and hide anywhere. Where would she go? Into the bathroom? Anyway, hiding wouldn't make him go away. She sensed that instinctively. He would simply wait until she was forced to emerge. In fact, she wouldn't put it past him to use starvation tactics if he felt it would assist his cause.

This, she knew, was an inflammatory situation. The air between them was tense, and whatever he was thinking it was obviously not to his liking, because his face was grim as it surveyed her.

'We need to talk,' he informed her shortly.

'Really?' Beth was rather proud of the fact that her voice did not betray what she was feeling, and she carried on coldly, 'I can't think of anything we could possibly have to talk about. And what about the party? Shouldn't you be getting back there? You're the boss, after all. As you've made clear to me on numerous occasions recently.'

'The party will survive without me,' he said abruptly.

'And Angela? Will she survive without you?' How she loathed that sharp, jealous edge to her voice. So much for her wonderful self-control.

Marcos shrugged carelessly, not taking his eyes off her face. 'She managed well enough before.'

'Good for her, but that won't be necessary because I don't want you here. It would be better if you left and——'

'Better for whom?' he enquired softly. He was standing over her now, and she craned her neck to look at him.

Better for me, she wanted to scream. Better if you just vanished in a puff of smoke and stopped turning my life upside-down whenever it suited you.

'I don't like talking here,' he said abruptly. 'Your sister might hear us, not to mention David, and I don't particularly relish having this conversation overheard.'

'There won't be any conversation,' Beth replied angrily. 'There won't be any conversation because there's nothing left to be said between us. It's all been said and it's pointless discussing any of it further. We had a brief affair, and now it's time we got back to our lives.'

'And what's your life?' Marcos muttered. 'Roger? Are you going to settle for second-best? A man you're not physically attracted to?'

Beth's eyes flashed. What did he want from her? Did he want to break down her defences completely by admitting that she was in love with him so that he could have the final laugh?

'I already told you that what I do is none of your business...'

'Well, it wasn't what I wanted to hear!' With a frighteningly quick movement he took her wrist and pulled her to her feet.

'Too bad!' Beth snapped back, wriggling against him and finally giving up the unequal struggle.

Her cheeks were flushed with confusion and anger, her lips half parted to frame a few more choice words on what he could do with his arrogance, when his head swooped downwards and he kissed her fiercely, his mouth crushing hers.

Beth fought and struggled against him, twisting her head to escape the burning, drugging ferocity of his kiss, but he was stronger than her and he had no intention of letting her go.

His mouth forced hers open and she felt a sickening elation as his tongue found hers, moving moistly against it.

'No!' she protested weakly.

She placed both palms against his chest to push him off, but it was like pushing against a steel barrier.

Finally he released her, and the unexpectedness of it made her sway on her feet. Before she could react, he lifted her up, carrying her across the room to the half-opened door to her bedroom, kicking it and then shutting it behind him. The light had been switched off before she had left for the party earlier on, and the darkness lent a strange intimacy to their situation.

Unable to see him clearly, she became intensely aware of his power. He had lifted her up as though she weighed nothing, and now he deposited her gently on the bed. Immediately she attempted to spring up, but he held her down, waiting until she had regained some of her composure before he spoke.

'We have to talk, Beth. Things can't go on like this. Dammit, woman, I have to know for sure what's going on between the two of you!'

'I thought you claimed to know it all!' There was silence. 'Will you leave if I give you your answer?' she asked desperately. More silence.

Maybe, she thought hopefully, his silence implied that he would. She needed him to. His presence here was like a net around her, making her unable to respond in the way that she knew she must. He had to leave.

She sighed heavily and then spoke. 'Nothing. All right? Is that what you wanted to hear? There's nothing going on between Roger and me. There never has been. He's a friend and that's all.'

This, she thought, was the final humiliation. It was tantamount to confessing that Marcos was the only man who could arouse her.

'Why didn't you tell me that the first time I asked?' he questioned roughly.

'Why should I have? It was none of your business. *I* was none of your business. Did I ask you what was going on between you and Angela?' She could not prevent the bitterness that had crept into her voice. It reverberated in the room, echoing back at her, reminding her how much power lay in Marcos's hands, power to hurt her.

'Nothing,' he said flatly. Suddenly he sounded bemused, as though he had been overtaken by some unexpected turn of event which he couldn't quite fathom.

It was all the more apparent because in every other aspect of his life he was always so much in command. He had an instinctive talent for knowing just how to play a situation, but now he was uncertain, attempting to grapple with a problem which was infinitely more slippery than he had bargained for.

Beth looked at him wide-eyed. Her eyes had adjusted to the darkness in the bedroom, but she could still only discern the shadowy outlines of his features.

'Do you really expect me to believe that?' she asked tightly, forcing herself not to succumb to the thrill of what he had admitted. 'Your idea of nothing going on must be very strange, because you two certainly seemed to have a lot of physical contact considering you claim that it was all a platonic relationship. What was that you said about body language?' God, she thought, her anger directed at herself, there I go again. Acting as though I own him when I know only too well that no one does.

'Dammit, Beth, I'm not lying. I don't understand it myself. No, maybe I do.' He looked away from her uncomfortably and raked his fingers through his hair with a frustrated groan. 'The fact is, nothing has happened between us. Not, I might add, for lack of trying on her part.' He laughed humourlessly. 'I wanted to get you out of my system, and I thought that the most effective way of doing that would be to replace you with another woman, but it didn't work. You see, you must have worked some damn spell on me, because I just couldn't respond to her. Any attraction between us—well, it wasn't there any more and there was no way that I could resurrect it.'

Beth felt a surge of joy rush through her. She smiled, and he must have sensed it because he immediately said, 'I suppose that makes you very happy, does it?'

'I suppose it does,' she agreed.

'Well, I hope that you spent lots of time suffering sleepless nights thinking about it, because that's what you caused me. Ever since everything blew up in my face, dammit. Ever since I walked into that office and saw you with Roger, I've been out of my mind with jealousy. I needed you to tell me that there was nothing between the two of you. God, I needed that more desperately than I wanted to admit to myself.'

He lay down beside her and stroked her hair, his actions gentle. The aggressiveness she had seen in him over the past few days had vanished.

How nice it would be, she thought sadly, to close my eyes and forget everything that has happened between us. To pretend that only the present matters. But she knew that it was an impossible dream. Even if he still desired her, she couldn't pick up the pieces of their affair and carry on.

She knew now with certainty that he meant too much to her. If she had to lose him, then it was better that she lose him now rather than make the same mistake of postponing the inevitable.

'There's no point to this,' she said shakily. 'I can't just hop back into bed with you. Too much has happened.'

'Do you want to hear me apologise for my behaviour?' Marcos asked huskily. 'I do. I was angry with you, I was angry with myself and most of all I was furious because I still wanted you when you should have meant nothing to me. Do you know how much my ego was dented by that charade of yours?' He laughed ruefully. 'I succeeded in a tooth-and-nail world, knew how to deal with the shrewdest of businessmen. No one had ever before pulled the wool over my eyes, yet there you were, calmly confessing to the biggest con I've ever witnessed.'

'I wasn't calm,' Beth pointed out.

'I felt like a complete fool,' Marcos went on. 'I'd met my match in you and I didn't like it.'

He sighed and pulled her against him, and for a minute everything flew out of her head except that peculiar warmth inside her, that stirring of her passions which only he could arouse.

He kissed her eyes, trailing his lips to hers, covering them with exquisite, teasing gentleness, until she thought that she would faint.

It isn't fair, she thought, it just isn't fair that one man can do this to me.

'Marcos,' she began unsteadily, 'I . . .'

'Don't talk,' he muttered, silencing her with his hand, which had found the zip at the back of her dress and was slowly releasing it, freeing her body from its textured prison.

He slowly pulled the top of her dress down and she wriggled out of it. He owns my body, she thought with sudden clarity. It no longer listens to what I have to say, it listens to his commands.

She had not been wearing a bra, and he caressed her smooth, naked breast with his hand.

'I spent hours imagining him touching you here,' Marcos murmured, his voice as unsteady as hers had been. 'I was tormented by the thought of it. There were times when I felt like I could hunt him down and rip him limb from limb. And enjoy every minute of it. Now do you understand what I meant when I told you that you had made me into a bastard? No woman had ever been able to arouse me to such a pitch of insane jealousy. In fact, no woman had ever come close. But you . . .'

He rubbed her nipple with his thumb and Beth groaned with excitement.

Somewhere in her mind, some hazy little voice was telling her about her principles, about her decision not to become involved with him again, but, try as she might, she could not summon up enough will-power to listen.

She stroked his face and then coiled her fingers into his hair, urging him to caress with his mouth what his finger had been caressing a moment before.

She felt the wet warmth of his mouth on her breasts, his tongue flicking over the aroused bud, sending darts of ecstasy through her.

He raised himself, and she was dimly aware of him removing his clothing, then he once more bent his head to her breasts, exploring every inch of them with rap-turous leisure.

'You have no idea how I've dreamt of this,' he whis-pered thickly. 'I felt sick with wanting it sometimes. When I saw you at the office, it was all I could do not to grab you and take you to the nearest hotel and make love. I spent hours reminding myself that you had de-ceived me, fighting that awful, primitive urge that re-fused to listen to reason.'

He eased her dress off completely, followed by her briefs, and she parted her legs to accommodate his ex-ploring fingers. Her body felt hot and feverish with passion. It was as though she had not made love with him for years.

'I want you, Beth,' he said huskily, kissing her mouth with tiny, hungry kisses. 'I can't tell you how much. More than words could ever express.'

Want, want, want, she thought with icy realisation. The word had dominated his conversation ever since they had returned to the flat. And she had been happy enough to go along with it.

But hadn't she already learnt from one lesson? Did she have to make the same mistake twice to realise that playing with fire entailed burnt fingers?

'I can't,' she whispered, turning away to hide the shine of tears in her eyes.

It took a few seconds for her words to sink in, then his body froze.

'Why not?' he demanded. 'I want you back. I need you to come back to me. Where's the problem?'

'The problem is me,' Beth answered fiercely. 'I know we've slept together, I know we've had our fling, but I can't accept that situation any longer.'

'And what's changed?'

'Nothing and everything.' Her nudity felt uncomfortable now and she drew the quilt around her, protecting her body from his searching eyes. 'I guess I always felt that way, but I was blind before. Now I know that I just can't.'

'After all that I've told you?' Marcos asked roughly.

'What have you told me? That you still want me. It's not enough.'

'Why not?'

She looked at him dumbly, unable to articulate all the myriad reasons why she could no longer be content to be wanted.

'Well, this is it, then.' He got up and slowly began putting on his clothes and Beth watched in silence, afraid to say anything in case she broke down completely.

Besides, there was nothing to say. This time it was final. In the morning she would leave for Cambridge and they would be free of each other. Except, lust was so much easier to surmount. He would recover from his so-called obsession with her in no time at all.

Whereas she . . . what would she do? Get another job, while away her time decorating her flat and dating pathetic little shadows of him? No man could ever be his equal. She would spend the rest of her years playing an endless game of drawing comparisons.

He began slipping on his shirt, then stopped and sat on the edge of the bed.

'Of course,' he said thoughtfully, 'but no. . .'

'"Of course but no" what?' Beth asked dully.

'Of course, we could get married.'

There was a long pause and she eyed him warily from under her lashes.

'Don't tease, please,' she whispered finally.

'Who's teasing? Believe me, I wouldn't dream of proposing to anyone unless I meant it.'

'You're proposing to me?' she said in a high voice.

Marcos glanced around the room then his eyes resettled on her face. 'Well, I don't see anyone else in here, do you?'

Beth didn't know whether to laugh or to cry. Neither could express the profound happiness spilling inside of her.

She sat up and flung her arms around his neck, settling for laughing, although her eyes were glistening.

'Does that mean that you accept?' he whispered, and she could hear the smile in his voice.

'What do you think?'

'Think?' Marcos looked down at her strangely. 'I lost the ability to do that competently when I'm with you a long time ago.'

'Good.' She pulled him down beside her and this time she undressed him, loving the feel of his skin under her fingers.

'Of course, you know what this entails. No more Roger.'

'But he's just a friend, and a good one at that!' she protested.

'He might get ideas if he's around you too much,' Marcos grated possessively. 'Maybe I can arrange a few more overseas projects for him.'

'A few more?' Beth raised one questioning eyebrow and he grinned.

'I didn't like him hovering in St Lucia. I think that was when it first hit home with me what you meant. I wanted you all to myself. When you had dinner with him, I spent the entire evening at my meeting over there brooding over what was going on. Whether you were holding hands over the aperitifs and staring romantically at each other over the main course.'

'You did?'

'I did, you little witch.'

Beth giggled with delight. His words filled her with a glow of happiness. 'Why didn't you say?'

Marcos shot her a rueful look. 'And admit that all my single-mindedness, my conviction that marriage was not for me, that women were enjoyable but not strictly essential, was down the drain?'

'You're admitting it now,' she pointed out logically.

'I didn't have much choice,' he muttered. 'Much as I hated it, I was forced to admit to myself that I was in love with you. Madly, blindly and infuriatingly in love with you.'

'What will Angela think?' she teased, nestling against him.

She felt him shrug. 'Oh, she'll get over me. I wasn't the first man she had slept with and I certainly won't be the last. No, women like Angela aren't easily crushed by an unsuccessful romance.' He paused and then asked, 'Were you jealous of her?'

Beth nodded.

'Say it!' he commanded.

'I was jealous of her,' Beth obliged. 'Desperately jealous. Every time I saw you together, something in me seemed to collapse.'

'Good.'

'You know, of course, that there can be no more Angelas.'

Marcos laughed under his breath. 'How could there be?' he asked. 'You've managed to trap me hook, line and sinker. You're the only woman I'm capable of seeing.'

She stroked his stomach and he sighed, covering her hand with his then running his fingers up her arm, trailing them delicately along her collarbone.

Beth closed her eyes, arching back as he kissed the white column of her neck, nibbling her earlobe, enjoying her quick, uneven breathing.

Her breasts pushed against his chest, the friction sending tiny shivers of desire through her.

He lay back, and she slid on top of him and he caressed her breasts with his hands, raising his head slightly to lick them.

Beth groaned. She wanted him; more, it felt, than she had ever wanted him before.

Because now there were no more barriers between them. Before, not even the intensity of their passion could quell the sickening knowledge that she was deceiving him, albeit against her will.

Now there was nothing to hide from him, and that seemed to liberate her, making her responses more abandoned than they had ever been.

'Beth, darling,' he whispered, pulling her down to him, kissing her on her lips, 'I can't hold on for much longer.'

This time she controlled the final rhythm of their lovemaking until their bodies were fused into one and she lost all sense of space and reality.

'My love,' he whispered huskily, turning to face her, 'I want to make you mine as soon as possible. No big white wedding. Something small, and preferably tomorrow.'

'Tomorrow?' she squeaked.

'Or very soon after.'

She looked at him thoughtfully and smiled. 'Well,' she said lazily, 'I suppose it's a good idea to be married quickly. After all, I'd like Laura to be there rather than miles away in a hospital about to give birth. Although, knowing my sister, she's sure to guarantee that things don't run that smoothly.'

She lay against him and thought of how shocked her sister would be when they broke the news to her in the morning. Shocked and delighted. Laura could be thoughtless, but her heart was in the right place, and besides it would be a weight off her mind knowing that Beth was happy, that her impulsive idea had not been an emotional fiasco for her sister.

She would sell her flat in Cambridge. The funny thing was that she had no regrets at the thought of doing so. Wasn't home where the heart was? Cambridge had ceased being her home the minute she'd met Marcos and fallen in love with him.

'You know,' he was musing next to her, 'I never thought Laura would have had the brazenness to concoct that plan of hers.'

'You just didn't know her. Believe me, if there's one person in the world who can concoct a plan like that, it's my sister!'

'Well, I was away for quite a bit of the time that she worked for me. In fact, I barely noticed her there at all. She was efficient, she obeyed my instructions without demur.' He chuckled and stroked her hair away from her face. In the darkness, her eyes met his and the breath caught in her throat as she glimpsed the tenderness in them.

'I should have realised that something was wrong when I first met you. You argued about everything.'

'Not everything!'

'Well, put it this way, you weren't backward at getting your point across, and it didn't seem to bother you in the least that I was your boss.'

'Should it have?'

'Whatever happened to respect?' He grinned with bemused admiration. 'No, I should have put two and two together, and at least suspected that something was wrong. After all, I suddenly began postponing trips away because I actually wanted to be in that damned office with you. Me! A man who had happily roamed the world for years, loving the freedom of having no ties!'

She pulled him towards her and kissed him firmly on the lips, and he stirred against her.

'Suddenly I found myself in a cage, and, worse, liking it!'

'You have the key to your cage,' she said quietly. 'You can leave now if you like.'

'Leave? You might as well tell me that I can fly to the moon, because I can no more leave than I can do that.'

'Poor Marcos.'

'You vixen,' he said fiercely, his leg covering hers, his hand outlining the smooth curves of her body. 'You're dangerous. I could spend a lifetime telling you how dangerous, and not come close to describing it.'

'No more talk,' she murmured. 'We have a lifetime together for that. Right now, let's just enjoy the moment.'

Beth looked at Marcos across the breakfast-table and smiled. The past eight months had been good ones. They had married quietly and honeymooned in Australia, much to her mother's delight.

'You married, and Laura settled with a baby—what a shame I'm not around to interfere,' she had joked.

Marcos looked up, caught Beth's glance and smiled back.

'What a pity I have to go to work,' he said softly, stirring her blood with the warmth of his gaze. Even now, one look from him still had the power to send her thoughts flying.

She no longer worked with him, instead devoting herself to the luxury of completing her book-keeping course, though some of the urgency behind it had been lost.

Laura was amused by it, but not nearly as amused as Beth was by her sister's decision not to return to work after the baby had been born. A bouncing boy who looked like a miniature clone of David.

'It's a pity,' Beth agreed, 'especially since you only have a limited time left with me.'

'What?' Marcos shot her a puzzled look, the dark eyebrows meeting in a frown.

'I mean, you only have a limited time left with me as I am.'

'Darling,' he murmured, coming across to her, kissing her on her lips with infinite care. 'I love you the way you are. There's no need to contemplate plastic surgery. In fact, I forbid it.'

He grinned and she giggled compulsively.

'Isn't it wonderful the way you laugh at my corny jokes?' he teased, caressing her with his eyes. 'It really must be love.'

'Well,' Beth said, sobering up, 'this is no corny joke. You're going to be a father.'

Marcos smiled slowly and shook his head. 'Already?'

'You said often enough that now that the yoke was around you, you might as well enjoy it, offspring and all.'

'So I did,' Marcos murmured, his smile broader now. 'Is that what you meant about no longer looking the same?'

Beth nodded. 'Expanding waistline is on the way,' she said, patting her still flat stomach.

'I've heard it said that pregnant women are very sexy.'

'Have you, now,' she joked.

'Just so long as it's my pregnant woman.' He placed his hand over hers in a gesture that was so painfully tender that it brought a lump to her throat.

'Are you happy?' she whispered.

'Happy?' Marcos chuckled softly. 'You gave me happiness when we met all that time ago, and you haven't stopped. As for going to work...'

He lifted her from the chair and she squealed in mock protestation.

'I think,' he murmured, 'a little celebration is in order.'

And it was.

HARLEQUIN®

PRESENTS: Plus

An affair...with her own husband? Laura and Dirk had
been separated but, all of a sudden, he was back in her
life and pursuing her. Laura couldn't forget that she had
been unable to conceive Dirk's child, which meant there
could be no long-term future for them—so why was she
still tempted to accept his simply *outrageous* proposal!

Nell was wary of men, until she met Ben Rigby and
found herself longing for something more. But she was
afraid. Her child—her lost child, whom she'd never had
the chance to see—shared the same birthday as Ben's
adopted son...was Fate being cruel or kind?

Harlequin Presents Plus—where
women's dreams come true!

Coming next month:

An Outrageous Proposal by Miranda Lee
Harlequin Presents Plus #1737

and

Shadow Play by Sally Wentworth
Harlequin Presents Plus #1738

Harlequin Presents Plus
The best has just gotten better!

Available in May wherever Harlequin books are sold.

⬥HARLEQUIN®

PRESENTS
RELUCTANT BRIDEGROOMS

Two beautiful brides, two unforgettable romances...
two men running for their lives....

My Lady Love, by Paula Marshall, introduces
Charles, Viscount Halstead, who lost his memory
and found himself employed as a stableboy by the
untouchable Nell Tallboys, Countess Malplaquet.
But Nell didn't consider Charles untouchable—
not at all!

Darling Amazon, by Sylvia Andrew, is the story of
a spurious engagement between Julia Marchant
and Hugo, marquess of Rostherne—an engagement
that gets out of hand and just may lead Hugo to
the altar after all!

Enjoy two madcap Regency weddings this May,
wherever Harlequin books are sold.